Canticle Mythos Series

Anthology II:

THE FIRST FALLEN

Limited Revised Edition.

Cover Art by Caelan Stokkermans / Illustrations by Abril Martinez
Logos, Maps by Maxwell Aston / Written by Matthew R.R. Morrese
Edited by Corwin Zahn / Published by Canticles Productions LLC
ISBN: 978-0-692-16868-4
12039 Avery Lane
Bridgeton, Missouri 63304

Accounts Recollected

by

Mimyr, the Second

Histories Penned

by

Matthew R.R. Morrese

Histories Edited

by

Corwin Zahn

Illustrations Brought to Life

by

Abril Martinez

The Limited Revised Edition is dedicated to all those
who prefer turning an aged page, rather than swiping
left on a silly screen, to all those who prefer driving to
flying, and to all those who prefer adventure and
romantics over apathy and rumination.
-MRRM

CONTENTS.

Concerning Mythology: In any mythology, we tend to focus on gods; in our case, the Eldûn – the Astar, the Ildraeor, and the Elzhri. Doing so lacks the proper time considered and thought given to that of "mortal man". The undying outshine the dying. Or, we focus on heroes and villains, an army instead of a soldier, the flock instead of a single sheep, the nameless that have been forgotten to time.

There were twelve races Aegis bore us, defined by their look, culture, religion, or civilized Realm, who appeared and evolved during the Age of Origin. Origin is defined as the first thousand years of Aegis' history – when the Ildraeor fashioned the scape of Her body, the Astar forged Her whispers into language, and the Elzhri, as nature-manifest, walked the world among mortals. The twelve races were nurtured by Aegis, and guided by these Eldûn, until Chaos bathed Her in bedlam's fire at Age's End.

Therefore, we take a step back from the names and numbers the Athenaeum's chroniclers collect, recount, and emphasize to look at those who played a role as individuals of lost memory, the little things and greater kinships that might have been lost if not for these tales. It was these peoples and races that gave Aegis Her meaning and purpose during the Age of Origin, because lives are so much more valuable if finite.

All tales are recounted here as best as we could avail them, as Mimyr herself sits afore me to help my hand along where I may forget. Consider this a reflection of our peoples. These are the First Sires.

E.

A Wreathelander's Wren

Old Man Cantor

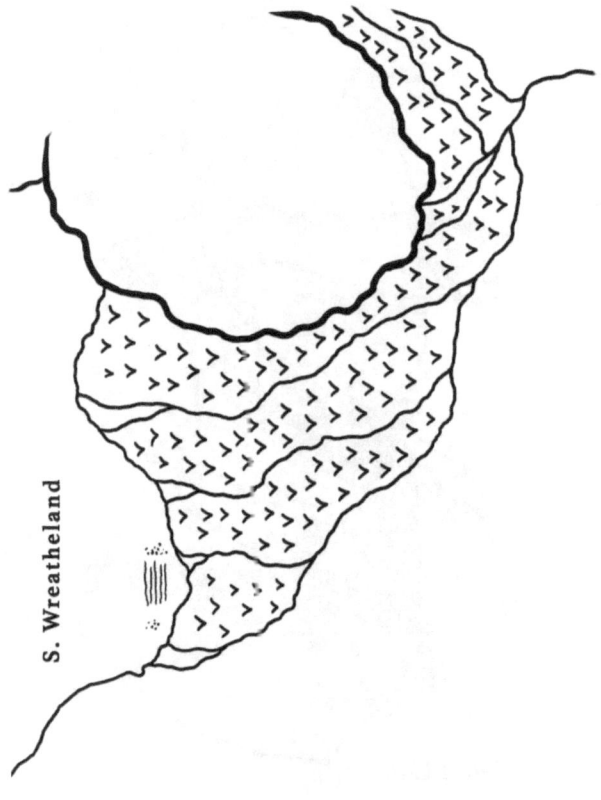

S. Wreatheland

...being a short story during the Age of Origin,
approximately in the year 500...

Old Man Cantor heard a trill on the wind, a breeze rising quickly into something fierce, a brooding distress that crept slowly into his elder bones. It whipped athwart the fields, increasing in strength as the Shadows grew longer across the land. Whatever dreadful thing threatened the Wreatheland this day, its nature was surely destructive.

The trill had an odd vibrato lacing its call, as if the throat releasing it was in terrible pain. He passed through the stalks of barley, rows of plenty nigh ready for the harvest, and paused every few feet to listen again for the unfortunate. His ears weren't what they used to be, and his son was visiting a friend in Fairfallow. For that, Cantor was on his own in this desperate search, and would be alone in the coming storm. Their herds were already panicked, but penned, and he'd seen the *lanser* flocks flee east, away from the darkening clouds now shifting in hue, a bilious green. The winds shifted direction, and the very scent of the air changed when he reached the edge of the field.

Disregarding all ill warnings, he finally spotted the wounded wren. It twittered from the ground where it lay, twitching its head back and forth – the poor bird knew a much larger one circled overhead, positioning itself for the kill. Cantor saw the deadly *kûros* – a bird of prey, hawkling descent – but surmised it wasn't what brought down the wren. More likely, it spotted the injured thing from on high and wasn't about to pass on a free meal. Luckily, Cantor, old as he was, hobbled over faster than the *kûros'* decision to dive. The old farmer knelt over the wren protectively, before the predator plunged.

The *kûros* wouldn't bother Cantor, so he took his time studying the wren's injury. Shielding the little creature from the rising weather, he saw the wren's right wing was broken, but not shattered – it could be mended, and healed in time. Again, the winds changed direction, but this time began to spin concentrically. They threatened to push Cantor down, but with forty years of farming behind him, he wasn't so easy to knock over. He gently scooped the wren into his palms, screening it as best he could from the winds. Slowly, he stood, spread his legs and bent his knees to steady himself. He trained his full attention on the sky. The temperature had dropped further, and the clouds bellowed and spiraled into what appeared to be a great toothless maw – he'd never seen anything like it, and knew he needed to get back to his house, now.

By the time he reached the porch, the wind had already ripped away the flag he flew deigning allegiance to Mistleton, the Wreatheland's capital center of commerce, trade and altogether industry of the Realm. Mistleton was where everyone sold most of their crop, and where he would if any of his own survived this unusual storm. It would be a difficult Dûntide if it didn't.

Priorities. He'd reached the house, and the little bird needed attention. The wren had relaxed in Cantor's palms since the field. He crossed into the foyer, found a rag and ripped it down to a twelve-inch strip. Fatherly, he wrapped the cloth about the bird to keep its body tight, but kept free its head and legs – it could breathe comfortably and didn't feel confined. He folded the wren's broken wing against the side of its body where it naturally fell; here, it kept the wing in place and at peace, but slipped under the unbroken wing about its breast so the poor thing could still balance with the functional one.

The windows rattled, and the walls shuddered. The rafters creaked; the roof moaned. Cantor looked up from his care, and his jaw dropped. Outside was something only the wrath of gods could have brought down – *have the Ildraeor been wronged this day?* He wondered. The storm clouds spun as a whirlpool in the sky, and a column of destruction touched down on the face of Aegis in a violent funnel that ripped up everything in its reach, an earthen squall tearing at Her flesh. This strange disaster, as if a weapon of the heavens, moved across the field slow and struck Graylor's place – the barn was there one moment, and in the next gone. He prayed his friend saw it coming. Cantor, sure as the Second, did – it was now coming straight for his fields, and his home.

The windows on his left shattered, bringing him back into survival mode – he clamped the wren between his palms, and raced through the house. There were things Old Man Cantor couldn't leave behind. He snatched up a burlap sack, hooked it to his belt, and tossed inside four things: First, his son's wooden knights, inherited from his father, and his father before him; second, the utensils his late wife crafted and carved by hand with which they supped each morning and night; third, a wreath of blown glass – a symbol of status across the Wreatheland – given to the Cantors by the Croparch of Mistleton; and fourth, a journeyman's canteen filled with water. The last thing he grabbed would not fit, and was not meant for the sack – it was an oar of his grandsire's, the first to take their family name down the South River Wreathe, a venture daring the very boundaries of the Wreatheland. His grandsire discovered the most fertile fiefs ever settled thereafter, and it was this plot that now marked the end of the Realm.

As the roof ripped away, Cantor dropped into a small wine cellar. It was as if the wings of Tûm'draeor herself bore down upon them. Inside the little sanctuary, he used the oar to bar the hatch, as the rest of the bunker was sunk into the earth on all sides. Then, he waited.

The echoing roar of turbulence outside the cellar grew in thunderous measure, until Cantor felt the earth quake all around him. Soil displaced and fell like rain washing over him, burying him. The hatch splintered and debris cut through his clothes and skin, but he clutched tight the wren, and shifted into a tighter clutch of hands and knees. He closed his eyes and prayed, *If I may die before the day, say you this unto my name: Fare thee well, and fare thee far, thy heart be freed of earth to star.* It was an old adage given to the dead, as he was very likely soon to be; however, he added to his prayer: *Earth-changer, skyborne, Tûm'draeor if it be you, may your wings take my land, but not the creatures who share your skies. Let this little wren be spared, and all those hearts that beat to serve only Aegis.*

A hollow cracking resonated the space, then bolstered into a howl as if a pack of *fyrwuhlfs* bayed in torment. He knew the oar split, and the door barring the cellar from the storm had torn. His back, exposed to the elements, was pelted with debris, bits and pieces of his own farm, his own house, his fallen home. The old man's hand shot out to find anything to hold onto – a root of some ancient tree that no longer grew here found his grasp. One arm held on for his own dear life, while the other held on to the wren's.

Young Man Cantor, the fifteen-year-old son of Old Man Cantor, returned to his father's fields the next day. The storm's ruin was all that remained, but optimism was always in the capacity of a Cantor; thus, he believed his father was here, somewhere, alive. After all, he couldn't rebuild all this on his own. He and his father would survive the aftermath of this catastrophe together, they would salvage what they could and erect a home even greater than the last. Some of the fields were destroyed, but the funnel itself was very precise in its direction, and left much of the harvest intact. Surprisingly the herds of goats and sheep and cattle, who'd escaped their pens when the winds blew apart the locks, had both run away and then promptly returned to their pastures. They would not let each other down – *chirp!*

He heard it faint against the snap of broken timber beneath his boot. Again, it came, much clearer. He waited for the third call, and with it pinpointed its location. He rushed over, knelt in the rubble, and dug. It wasn't long before his fingers bled, but all he felt was the need to find his father alive.

The call grew louder and louder through the still air, and he began to fear nothing was beneath the rubble but a flock of trapped birds. Then, with a mighty groan, Young Man Cantor heaved the final stone displaced from somewhere far away and fallen here by the winds to reveal his father, buried alive, but living. He rolled over and coughed, "About time, m'boy. We've got work to do."

Old Man Cantor gave the last drop of his canteen's fill to the wren, then unwrapped the little bird. It was a cycle past the storm the Wreathelanders named the *taerkrathi* – a wrathful bite of wind and rain that released from the skies in a spiral to tear up flatlands for a surprisingly short amount of time. He and his son spent the moonstide rebuilding what they could, a structure well-enough off to last them through the Withering Season and Ilaeon. In the end, they'd survive.

Cantor watched the wren hop up and down, bristle its feathers, and stretch its wings. In no time, it lifted into the air on the slightest, helpful current. He thought on that for a moment and chuckled. The wren flew south, "To fairer winds, I hope," he called out to it, "And may fairer weather greet us all in the season to come." He looked back at his son, and smiled, "We'll last to the last, eh?"

An Elvar's Trial

Ekendör Ko Ûroshyr

Eastern Pass

...being a short story during the Age of Origin,
approximately in the year 707...

"You're making a mistake," the traitor replied, undeterred by the arrival of the executioner.

Ekendör Ko Ûroshyr looked down on her from his seat as High Arbiter. "The tribunal has spoken," he stated softly; he didn't agree with the sentence, but the citizen jury ruled in cases of sanctimony. There was nothing he could do but pass the sentence. "Under the Elvar's Edict, you crossed a line. Poor judgement led to gross misconduct. That misconduct resulted in what we can call no less than purposeful sacrilege against the Sacred Steps. You defiled our holiest of peaks, allowed foreigners to scar its stone, burning it with the savage eyes of lessers. You are found guilty of dereliction in your sacred duty to keep hidden the secrets of the Evarseer. Now, we must all live in fear for our lives in the ever-likely scenario the Baymen lead something terrible to our gates."

The blasphemer was gently pushed up the steps of the scaffolding into position upon the gallows. It was a standing structure Ekendör had always despised, threatening guilt before innocence. She began the plea he knew would come, "I trust them; we think too low of—"

"This is a sentence," Ekendör interrupted, "A discussion no longer. You will respect it." He had expected her plea to be for herself, not the savages.

"You have more to fear from the *evari*—"

"Silence!" the command echoed across the empty space. The Hall of Judgement was a large cavern in the belly of Mount Syrsin, at the center of the *Evar-aeor Ritûm*, and the heart of Elvar society across the range. As for her supplicating attempts, Ekendör need not to hear it again. His own doubts on the matter already threatened his every word; he had no desire for this to be any harder than it already was. For either of them.

A soldier appeared from the Shadows of a hall set directly behind the stone seat. He whispered in Ekendör's ear, "We found them, Arbiter. They're still on the coast, making ready their sails."

Ekendör nodded, emotionless, but the guilty far below guessed the message:

"Please, don t!" she cried up.

Ekendör thought the enemy lost, as a fortnight had already passed since Lieutenant Ûrotûm Ka made them all aware of the crime.

Something must have delayed the pirates, fortunately for the Elvar. "Send a jack to our northeastern outpost. Take them, now."

As the hemp lowered around her neck, the prisoner continued to plea not for herself, but for the two Baymen she'd befriended: "One of them is paralyzed for 'zhri's sake!" The executioner fitted the noose about her neck, but she would not be phased. "They are not the enemy!"

The executioner placed his hand on the release lever to the trap at her feet and waited for the arbiter's signal. Without hesitation, Ekendör raised his hand, "Whatever you saw was a lie. In them, or in the stars. You are too young to understand, and my heart breaks that you may not be allowed further understanding. May the Seventh's mantle wash over your Shadow peacefully." His hand fell, and with it the executioner's grip tightened. He pulled the lever down its fateful descent, and the floor dropped from beneath the criminal's feet.

Unfortunately, that was not the end.

The rope sprang back just before she hit the ground and snapped taught, measured perfectly to give the crowd excitement. However, there was no crowd today. He forbade it. Her muscles contracted immediately. Her legs flailed, and her body wriggled. She used every breath left to her to warn her people: "The gods will fail – guilt will consume them!" she choked through the cruel grasp of death. The hemp pressed mercilessly on her elegantly long, but muscled esophagus; she could no longer take in new breath. "Let them be! Darkness is coming!" She fought, but nothing else escaped her lips. Nothing else could.

She kept her eyes trained on Ekendör as the seconds dragged on, tormenting him. In the end, it took nine minutes for her to hang still. In the end, his guilt settled as a noose around his own neck. And in the end, Evendir Ko Ûrotyr was killed for no reason other than fear and pride, and her grandfather found he suddenly couldn't breathe.

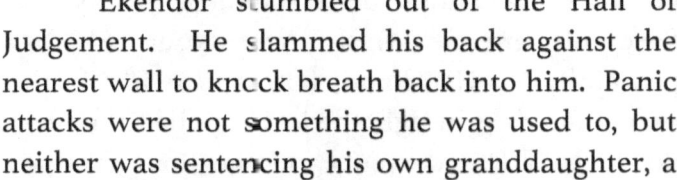

Ekendör stumbled out of the Hall of Judgement. He slammed his back against the nearest wall to knock breath back into him. Panic attacks were not something he was used to, but neither was sentencing his own granddaughter, a child, to death. He slowly regained composure and steadied his breathing.

The tribunal was set in their paranoia, steadfast to a superiority complex above all save for the gods themselves. On paper, she was a traitor, and that's all that mattered to them where their religion was concerned.

Now, only the two Baymen were left. They
would be caught and tried the same, but he prayed
they'd be killed before they ever got there. They
surely wouldn't go without a fight. He wanted
nothing to remind him of this day, and wanted
nothing more than this trial to disappear into the
annals of history.

For days, Ekendör wandered the Elvar's
Realm aimlessly, from the pools in the depths of the
ritûm to the broad glades set along wide
escarpments around the range's peaks. Many of
their homes were built within the mountains, in
halls similar to that of Judgement, each one erected
as a community of families with a communal well
at their centers; however, most of their activities,
and all of their agriculture, was laid out between
mountains in the Evar'aeor's valleys, vast and lush
with natural resource. They were quite blessed,
actually.

The arbiter played it over and over again in
his mind. Evendir's death was wrong. He knew
that. But, what of tradition? Of law? He'd thought
of visiting the *evarik* to ask the stars for guidance, to
take a pilgrimage of reflection up to the peak of the
Evarseer, but he knew he would only find himself
closer to the inner turmoil that ravaged his heart,
now. Nothing but his own acceptance of this act

would lead to forgiveness. He didn't want to believe there was anything he could've done to change it. *Was there?*

Today, he found himself at the eastern gate. It marked the edge of Elvar lands and bordered the Embers against the Zhrizûr Divide. He'd never been out this far in his long-lived life, and wondered what had taken him there today, what was beyond the place all Elvar called home. It was a narrow passage between Mount Lûmdöt and Mount Lûmdir. He stood at what he guessed was a mile in from the inner lock to their world for a long while. Two guard towers rose at the lock, barbicans crenelated and looming over any who might seek entrance or make siege. As his thoughts trained on these spires of strength, menace, grandeur, he saw four figures emerge from the Shadow. The guards sent to apprehend the Baymen had returned.

As his granddaughter had tried to make clear during her trial, one appeared paralyzed from the neck down, an injury sustained during the battle Evendir claimed was a misunderstanding in the Lûmrik'aeon. Evendir had paralyzed the man in a turn of desparation, acting for the benefit of all, and doing her holy duty at the time to protect their home. She should have finished the job, but she'd decided to spare them when the other Elvar present, Ryrenkûr, was disabled himself. This sparked a ridiculous truce at the time.

The pirate's mate carried the paralyzed, now. In addition to the hard venture they'd made in and out of the mountains already, they were both well weathered and battered, worn from years at sea. The lame had a matte of black hair with a heavy set of whiskers, while the one who carried him had a startlingly bright red mane with fairer skin, too young possibly to grow anything but whiskers. Ekendör stayed put and allowed the troop to reach him.

They halted then, and the two soldiers bowed with respect and similar surprise. One of them began cordially, "High Arbiter, what brings you so far?"

Ekendör was familiar with the soldier, a loyal clan to the Watchers. "Just following my feet," he feigned a smile, "I see you've returned, punctual as always Rösken. Injuries?"

"They surrendered," Rösken scoffed.

"We did?" the paralyzed Bayman piqued, "I thought *you* surrendered t'*us*. If not, we should pro'ly take our leave, eh cap'n?"

Ekendör doubted the supporting man, no more than boy, could be a captain. And while he was clearly exhausted, he matched the jocularity, "I think we should. Total misunderstandin'." He made to turn, but Rösken shot out his arm to bar the way.

"We were just taking them to the cells, sir."

"I will take them from here," Ekendör answered, surprising himself.

Rösken bustled, as he should've, "I'm... I'm not sure you have the authority, respectfully, sir. These are dangerous men, whatever demeanor they may carry. They're savages."

"Yes. They are," Ekendör agreed. The soldier shouldn't let him take the men, but, in the end, he would. "But, right now, I fear more for the safety of our sanctuaries than wasting soldiers on a brute realmsbent on supporting his lame kin. He is lame, is he not? If they got word to Ildûron, we could be facing a dire future sooner rather than later. The entire Evar-aeor is on alert, and we need all the eyes we can muster."

Rösken looked at his partner patrol, then unhooked a secondary belt from his thigh, "Take this, sir, just in case. I'll get another back at the tower."

Ekendör nodded, and took the belt, strapping it to his own thigh. After making sure the blade was secure, he led the Baymen forward. They walked a good hundred feet or so in silence. When the soldiers were out of earshot, the arbiter looked at his feet, but spoke surely, "Your lives have been pled for by the dead."

It took a few more steps before the information sank in. The lame pieced it together first, "Ya killed her?!"

"Marryk," the so-called captain soothed him. Marryk silenced immediately, and swallowed further comment. There was still a chain of command between the two. However, the boy stopped in his tracks, forcing Ekendör to do the same.

When the arbiter turned to the pirates, he decided to face it head on, "Yes. We did. She broke the law, many times in fact, in the very short period her curiosity of you tainted her. Thus, she was tried and sentenced to hanging."

"Curiosity leads to a fatal sentence?" the boy asked, bewildered, "I was startin' to believe you people were alright."

"Her decisions led her to the noose. She could have stayed her curiosity before it led to sacrilege. She desecrated our most holy sanctum."

"Pretty sure that was us, not her."

"If it weren't for her, you'd already be dead."

"Even on the seas, we ain't so harsh."

Ekendör sneered, "I find it hard to believe you people have laws at all." He tried to move forward, but the Baymen stayed where they were.

"Few of 'em, sure, just a few articles, really," he shrugged, "But they're fair. Are ya takin' us back for a similar ritual suicide? 'Cause, somethin' tells me we have little chance of acquittal."

Ekendör was hard pressed to believe this boy was so intelligent. He spoke well for a pirate, and held himself confidently. Ekendör knew the moment he took them back, they would be found guilty, and they'd suffer worse than hanging. *Why have I decided to take them?* "What are you?" He wasn't sure what other titles there were on a seafaring vessel, but, "So young. You can't be a captain."

"I am. That's what 'appens when everyone else dies."

"Alright, captain," he submitted politely, calm, a judge through and through. "Tell me, if your trial was here, now, what reason would you give a tribunal to live, to plead for your lives after the secrets you've seen?"

Neither responded right away. Marryk knew when to wait for his captain. At length, the red-haired boy set Marryk on the ground and responded calmly, but accusingly, a tone hard with his own judgement, "Our trial? Here? This is not *our* trial. 'Cause ya've already decided what to do wit'us, to keep secrets that we couldn't care less about. Nah, Elvar. Nah. This is yer trial. This is when the gods judge *you*. The woman ya killed ... by the end, we called'er friend, and knew not why we ever called her enemy. She was innocent. Me and mine? We ain't innocent. We're pirates, sure as can be. We came to take yer relics, steal yer treasures, that's the truth. 'Cause we thought ya a myth, a legend, a ghost story. What 'appened down in that cove ... things change. And the road we took together ... we carried our burdens, the both of us, and we learned. Maybe ya haven't been given that chance, how could ya? But, I'll say this. If ya want to sentence us for what we've done ... let me confess to ya..."

Ekendör saw the tears well up in the man's eyes; he was remembering, remembering a past he loathed, but accepted.

"...Let me confess to ya the men I've killed and the pearls I've stolen in m'years at sea. Let me tell ya of the ships I've burned and towns I've sacked in the wars 'tween Embers and 'Hearth." He paused here, making certain Ekendör was listening well. At length, he stepped forward, and gazed up into the eyes of the Elvar. Somehow, his accent cleared, and he spoke more like a Reignmen, than Baymen, "Do not sentence me for something I have not yet done. We will not tell yer secrets, wondrous as they are, but be sure we will tell of you – an unforgiving people, who would sentence the

23

innocent to die, because she tried to understand someone before judging them. 'Oh, be warned!' I'll say, 'fer if ya cross the path of the Star-folk, you'll likely burn in the wake of their own curiosity.' Let the gods be witness to that if they will, and kill us now."

Ekendör found himself speechless after such a diatribe.

"One heck of a goin'-out speech, cap'n."

"Thanks, Marryk," the boy smiled.

Ekendör knew if he let them go, he would meet the same fate as his granddaughter. *How can everything be so turned around?* The Elvar focused so much on the knowledge and wisdom given to them by the stars. But, reading the mantle of the *evari* was the future, and the here was now. He had the power to change this, even if he didn't want that power. "You saw our secrets," Ekendör spoke at last, "Our land. Our people."

"Aye," the captain nodded, slipping back into his pirate tongue. "And fer whatever it's worth, it was worth every minute t'see this world from yer ... *evarik*." He addressed Marryk, "That what she called it?"

As he was paralyzed, Marryk's voice was only laced with the essence of a shrug, "I was distracted, sir."

"I would see yours, now," Ekendör said plainly.

The Baymen's eyes showed surprise as one, and neither hid it well. Marryk chose to answer, to push, "The seas're no place for Elvar."

Ekendör cocked a wry smile at the paralyzed, "When one has resolve, one finds resistance to tribulation. Eh?"

The captain cocked a wry grin, "Aye, then. But, somethin' tells me the guards won't allow us back out that way."

"There are many ways in and out of these mountains, boy; after all, they're just mountains." He offered his hand in a general greeting he knew was used by the Baymen of the Embers, "Ekendör Ko Ûroshyr."

"Always so fancy," he smiled back, and took the hand firmly. "*Captain* Dyn Kaird of the late *Bighter's Wrath*. And this is my first mate – well, my only mate – Marryk. Don't think there's a surname. Is there?"

"Nope," Marryk shook his head.

The two Baymen were led under the mountain's Shadow by the High Arbiter, an Elvar guiding his lessers to freedom.

Anthology II

A Bayman's Odyssey
Part 1

Marryk, First Mate & Friend

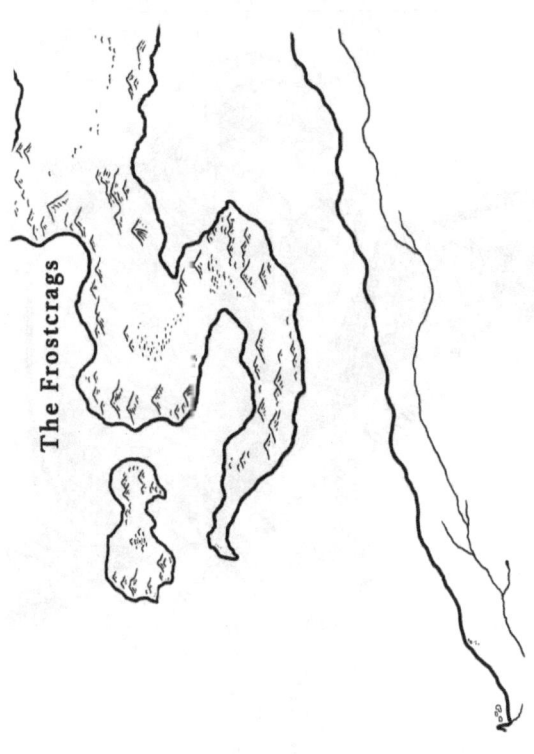

*...being a short story during the Age of Origin,
approximately between the years 707 – 717...*

Three days of fair winds and clear skies ended abruptly. The clouds were now gray, and a light rain hit the deck. *Is it even a deck?* Dyn thought, scratching the bright red stubble, growing uneven and rampant across his face. Their vessel was no more than driftwood – pieced, pegged, and lashed together with ivory cord. They'd spent a week hunting to exhaustion before the seal-skin stretched the entire length and width of the raft; however, Dyn was forced to steal the oils used to coat and waterproof the seams from a local fishing village. *It's what I'm good at – stealing – I'm a pirate, after all.*

Luckily, Dyn Kaird finished all this preparation before they were awkwardly abducted by the Elvar soldiers, only to be freed again by their enemy, turned ally, before they could be put on trial. When they returned to the raft, the oils were dried, and the ship was as good as it was going to get with pursuers on their heels. The Elvar were the reason travelling by land wasn't an option. The Baymen were seafaring by nature, but Dyn guessed the Elvar had never built a boat in their history beneath the mountains. Strange as this was, one oddly natured fellow was along for the ride – Ekendör Ko Ûroshyr, the Elvar that was meant to sentence them to death, but found his conscious instead. This Star-Folk claimed he wanted to "expand" his knowledge of a Realm his people believed they were above, but Dyn had to wonder if there was some ulterior motive.

Their course was to kiss the coast all the way to Ildûron. This way, they could anchor anywhere along the way to resupply; the raft wasn't big enough to store meat or fresh water past a certain point, and there was no telling how long this journey would take.

He held the oars – the longest, straightest, flattest limbs they could find at the time – tight, and looked up, past their single mast of woven wool he'd pulled off beached and broken ilk, to the sky. There was no time to anchor before the storm hit, and, in the moonlight, through the thin, misting clouds hovering low and lower, he couldn't quite understand what he was looking at: "In all'r years at sea, mate, 'ave we seen the like?"

Marryk, his first and last mate, shook his head – it was the only part of his body left with motor function by their first run-in with the Elvar, and the female called Evendir. The paralyzed man grew similarly confused, "Ne'er, cap'n."

The old Star-Folk with them lifted his eyes from a journal in his hand, "Is it unnatural for sea rocks to do that?"

Ahead of them, spires of rock lilted in the sea, columns of continent separated before time began, now bobbed up and down, side to side, with the fury of a growing, roiling tide. They were never in the same place twice; they grazed across each other in quick, temporary collisions before they pulled away again in constant shift. This peculiar, devilish reef extended into the deepening waters as far as they could see. Marryk, with the eyes of a master-harpooner, observed this obvious account for his captain, "No goin' round 'em, sir."

"Eken," Dyn shortened the Elvar's name for haste. "I'm glad yer with us. Can ya take the rudder there, and steer? If not, I'd like ya to return those senses yer people took from m'mate 'ere."

"I believe I can steer," Ekendör replaced the journal to his robes, and clasped the pocket tight; he shifted to the rudder.

Marryk attempted levity, "So, who do we pray to? To pass 'em before that storm hits us?"

The scent of the storm wafted over them, now – it wouldn't be long. "Let's go with the Sixth, eh? If we die, I wanna lover's embrace in the Deep."

Dyn feared for both the integrity of the raft in a storm, but moreso the clashing rocks. He'd fought storms before – hundreds of times, in fact – but, he'd never faced a phenomenon like this. *Will I meet the same fate as you, Byrbor? Or, in death, has your luck passed onto your cabin boy?*

The sister-moons of Aegis dipped in and out of the rainclouds as they hit the reef's perimeter. Marryk guided them with his eyes, Ekendör directed them with the rudder, and Dyn drew on every bit of strength he had to propel them through each tide, twist, and turn by oar.

A smaller boulder scored their underbelly, "Away, away!" Marryk called, and Eken obeyed, turning them farther from the coast. "Steady..."

Two spires collided behind them; Dyn snapped the oars out of the water, and let them ride the wave. "Starboard!"

A spire smashed into their starboard; Eken called, "What direction is that?"

"Right," Dyn answered. "Right!"

"Left," Marryk continued, and, this time, Eken succeeded.

Dyn returned the oars to the water, "Fine, let's not use 'em sea-farin' terms, eh?"

"Left – Right – More right!" Something very large loomed, "Away!" but it was too late, and

Eken's reflexes were not a young Elvar's anymore. He was an elder, who'd spent the last century on the judiciary committee.

While they skirted around the rocks to port, the ones at bow came in hard, smashed into them, and cracked the timber keeping them afloat. This may have not been detrimental if the oar there hadn't been taken out as well. "I guess we're relyin' on the current!" Dyn cried, and moved back to lend a hand at the rudder.

Another series of shouts from Marryk got them past another dozen deaths, and Dyn spotted the end. Just before they cleared the clashing rocks, a spire shot from the depths of the sea, scored their port side, and threw them into another. Their aft was struck, and the rudder splintered away.

"Hold on, Elvar!" Dyn cried. While Marryk was tied upright to the mast, he and Eken were not. They grabbed hold of the ropes lashing the raft together, and held on for dear life through torrent and current.

When the waters suddenly calmed around them, Dyn lifted his head, and looked behind them. They'd left the columns of catastrophe behind; unfortunately, they were also dead in the water.

That's when the rain began to fall harder. He thanked the Sixth for the timing, but cursed the

Realm for the outcome he should've expected – one trap had led them to another.

A battered carrack was anchored to the shallows afore them, run aground the rocks. By Dyn's perspective it did not look sailable – shrouds in shreds, foremast collapsed, and spotty patchwork done in many places across the hull; however, it did look like it was waiting to take advantage of any survivor of the rocks. Aboard that ship would be the worst kind of pirate there was – scavengers. Granted, all they had was their three lives, but Dyn knew Baymen had no quarrels or morals against slavery. They would outright kill Marryk on account of his disability, sell Dyn for a fair price to a coastal reef farm, and they would either revere Eken or torture him for all he knew of Elvar secrets. "Well, that ain't good," quipped Marryk.

"Should we not count ourselves lucky for being alive?" Eken asked.

"Jury's still out on that one, judge."

It didn't take long for the current to close the gap, between their floundered raft and the decrepit carrack. In faded paint, its name read *The Wiles*. "Doesn't seem so dramatic," Marryk thought aloud.

A harpoon struck the wood next to Marryk's legs. He would've jumped if he could. They felt a jolt, heard a slow, echoed creaking from the vessel's deck, and were reeled in. When they bumped against the hull of the *Wiles*, nothing happened, and everything went still. They were expected to board on their own accord.

"They expect us t'meet our own fate," Dyn explained to the Elvar's curious stare. "We can climb, or try swimmin' to shore." On cue, there was a deafening roar from somewhere along the mountains. "They'll take us the easy way, or enjoy huntin' us down."

"Barbaric."

"Yeah? So's hangin' the innocent." Dyn answered, referring to Evendir, Eken's own granddaughter he'd sentenced to death for helping the very pirates he accompanied now. "All peoples got a side they're not proud of; but, in this case, we have no choice. We can't get Marryk ashore, and I won't leave him." It was a point and decision already made and settled before Ekendör decided to help them, so the Elvar knew better than to question Dyn's honor, now. Realistically, he saw it very little in the seat he held over so many others in the Elvar court, so it came as a relief this pirate bore some altruistic code.

Dyn looked to Marryk, but didn't have to ask.

Marryk nodded, "Go, cap'n." He smiled, "I'll be waitin'." Again, he was the only one who kept to levity in the dire situation, and Dyn appreciated it. *When your mind is all you have, I suppose you have to.*

Dyn nodded and addressed the portholes, "Keep yer ears open, friend. Ya never know." Dyn rose and moved to a series of rungs that led up to the deck. He ascended, and Ekendör followed.

When Dyn peered over the rail, he couldn't believe his eyes. "Eken, has my jaw hit ya down there?"

"If you are referring to the turn of phrase for surprise, I cannot say, but – physically – no. However, if you will let me up, we may find your jaw together."

Was that a joke? Dyn didn't have the time to figure it out. He pulled himself over the rail, Eken followed, and both stood on the weather deck of the carrack, staring in awe at the sight afore them.

A crew of women stared back – six across the deck, two from the rigging, and another from the nest – all dastardly attractive. Each had red locks of Baymen true, with leathers and weapons that matched their station aboard the wreck. Dyn had heard tale and fantasy about pirate women that sailed to seduce men at sea before devouring them, their bodies or their gold (or both), but he'd never seen one in person. Now, there was an entire crew of what Baymen legends called piresses. Luckily, it wasn't lost on Dyn that every pair of eyes was on his comrade.

Slow, casual, Ekendör about-faced, knowing his place, and whispering down a reminder to the lad, "Do not forget your own people. Or more importantly – mine."

Dyn *had* forgotten. Dyn Kaird, and the crew of the late *Bighter's Wrath,* were the only Baymen who'd ever come into contact, or even real proximity, with one of the Star-Folk for longer than a brief sighting or quick offering. *Marryk and I might be the only outsiders to ever know who they really are – just a people, like any other, with faults and failings of their own.* Baymen, as a whole, as a society and civilzation, still saw the Elvar as greater, placed them on a pedestal the Star-Folk erected through years of Embermyth; they were clouded in histories manipulated by the Elvar themselves. In fact, to most, they were nigh as gods in Baymen lore – *Ridiculous!* He thought about it, but that carefully woven chicanery may be the only thing that could save them now.

A piress with numerous braids falling to waist height was the first to speak in a hushed, almost reverent tone, "Are you ... Elvar?"

Dyn immediately started formulating a plan. *I hope this comes to fruition – I have no idea what*

I'm saying, "Aye," he stepped between them, "M'lady piress," he bowed.

"And you are?" one of the reds from the rigging called down to the point.

"His servant. His tongue. T'is lessers." He decided to speak a little more broken than his usual Ember accent; if they thought him uneducated, they would underestimate him, surely. He already knew what they would ask next, and didn't waste time getting there, "M'ship was destroyed by yer rocky friends back 'ere, and I thought I's drown-ed when..." He paused for effect. "When a hand from the swirling mists," he looked down at his own, an actor in a play, "amidst the clashing spires, appeared 'ere, and pulled me aboard. The great Elvar'd already saved one man just moments 'fore. I was the second. The raft ya drew in was 'is, and he's his own story to tell." If they asked, Dyn knew Marryk would come up with something fanciful. "Only with the guidance of the Great Reader of Stars did we make it alive – miracle, to be sure, and I'll thank'ee holiness every day I now serve'im."

Braids spoke up again softly, "Why would the great Elvar go to such lengths to save you."

"Can't say, lass," Dyn drooped his head, "Said us worthy. Said he be studyin' those like us, to understand better we who worship 'em."

Silence. All but for the tide gently splashing over the reef, it fell and lasted. He was never bad at improvising, but a lot of this would hinge on Ekendör playing his part as well.

The mysteries of the Elvar won out, but Dyn's hope for a simple solution grew complicated, and confusing, when Braids stepped up cautiously past Dyn. "Would his holiness help our cause as well, then?"

Ekendör cocked his head back, but did not look down at her. He did not have to feign curiosity, but he played the part of nonchalance perfectly, allowing Dyn to answer:

"What ails yer ilk, piress?"

"Our last engagement 'pon the sea was five years past. Heavily damaged, we were run aground and left for dead. The Fire-Guzzler himself, if you know the name."

Dyn did, and it took all he had to keep from laughing. It was he, Captain Byrbor, Fire-Guzzler, Bed-Breaker, who Dyn served under as cabin boy. It was under his command, and his ambition, he and Marryk found themselves the last of his crew, on this heart-breaking odyssey. He wasn't sure where the term came from, but knew it meant a long, arduous series of hardships one could attribute to poetic adventure. Byrbor went out magnificently, an end worthy of his name, but took too many with him in that bloody cove. The piress didn't need to know any of this, of course. "He just left ya 'ere?"

"He heard the monster's roar, and fled." She stepped back, realizing addressing Dyn was the only option. "Whereas our captain struck a deal with the beast, and that peace has lasted so long. We bring it food, and we aren't the next meal. For whatever the sight of it, we've made the ship sailable again, but we fear any attempt at breaking free of the reef will incur the wrath of old Skyra."

Dyn hadn't heard of the creature, but saw Eken's fist clench. "Are ya askin' the Holy Lord t'ssuage this creature," he covered, chuckling at the absurdity, "or slay it for ya?"

Braids looked back up at the Elvar, daring as she was, "Surely, those who are said to control the very stars themselves can control a vile monster of their mountains."

Ekendör whirled around with just enough dramatic flourish – snapping his robes like a whip – to force each piress to take a reverent step back, though they couldn't say why. The Elvar spoke in a low voice, deep enough to spook them and resonate over the deck: "Do not presume your lives are worth more than the creature your captain bargained with, girl."

Braids bowed her head, "I apologize, your holiness. Forgive me. It has been ... a long wait for a miracle."

"Then don't wait for one." Ekendör walked gracefully, almost gliding to the rail facing the rocky shore. "I know She of whom you speak. She is powerful, beautiful, deadly." Ekendör turned back and stared at Braids, intimidation burrowing deep, "And she has called this coast home longer than your pitiful band of brigands in their little boats have been pillaging it. You sicken me."

Dyn could feel the tension spreading, and could only hope he hadn't taken it too far. No one knew what to make of the Elvar, what to believe, or what to say. Therefore, Dyn followed his lead, "Yer 'oliness, may I suggest ya give 'em only godly guidance at first. Read the stars, perhaps, and pass on their knowledge, if they even this worthy? These piresses may at least repent on their actions, if not act on their own."

Eken appeared to catch his drift. Dyn was telling him they needed to stall. "Agreed," he said at length. "At emberfall, the *evari* will decide your worth. As we wait for the flame to fade, you will bring the other man aboard. He, too, as my servant has stated, owes me his life. Give him fresh clothes, and wash the soiled ones. Then, hitch him to your ... crow's nest," it was as if he wasn't sure of the word, but found it in time not to raise suspicion – the Elvar were not a seafaring folk. "His eyes will keep watch on those mountains better than any of you. Pray that Skyra is not hungry tonight, and take me to your captain."

"Of course," Braids said, bowing her head, "Of course. And thank you, great one."

"She is always hungry," the red on the rigging quipped as Eken was taken away. "Always."

Dyn was shown to the cabin girl's quarters by Braids. "Laeryn," she introduced herself, "Quartermaster."

"Is yer cabin ... girl, I presume, absent?" Dyn asked.

"Nay, she was fed to the creature." She easily read Dyn's surprise. "Sometimes, there is a lack of bodies floating in from the clashing rocks; therefore, we've had to be creative in servicing her."

"Yer cap'n is cruel."

"We do what we must to survive."

"I's cap'n of a crew once, before me own misfortune. Yer crew is yer family, thicker than blood. So, I repeat, yer captain is cruel."

Laeryn didn't argue; it was obvious she didn't agree with the decision, but things were done at sea every ship wasn't proud of. She left him there alone, but he heard her lock the door – he was no

Elvar, and would not be treated with any more respect than a prisoner. In fact, he was pleasantly surprised at his quarters, as he expected a cell in the brig. The hold was much like his own cabin aboard the *Bighter's Wrath*, a saddening honor to remember it all. Thinking back, he realized it wasn't so long ago that it all fell apart, that he went from cabin boy to captain to survivor. The hammock tugged at his desire; he wanted to relax, sleep, just a wink, but knew he shouldn't. There was no rest to be had here, not until they were safe. And he knew what he needed to find – another blessing for the quarters Laeryn assigned him.

Every cabin boy, or cabin girl in this case, held the ship's Articles for their captain. This ship was surely no different than every other across the Bight. The only place for them was a small desk with a single drawer, and he knew there'd have been no reason to move them while beached. The drawer was locked, but Dyn was as good as any other with his lot in life at picking it. He found a pin among the cabin girl's accoutrements, and picked the lock quick and clean.

The drawer popped open, and he pulled out the papers, laws governing *The Wiles*. Most of these were similar among pirate vessels, but never two the same. Therefore, he read them over and over until memorized. The details were the difference, and it would be the details that could free them if Eken wasn't convincing the captain right now to just let them go.

The Articles read:

I.   *Every woman has a vote in the affairs of the Company, and receives equal title to the fresh provisions and liquors seized, to be used at pleasure, unless a scarcity makes it necessary to ration.*

II.   *Stealing from the Hold is punishable by marooning. If the robbery is betwixt one another, it is to be settled on deck by duel to first blood.*

III. *No person is to game at cards or dice for anything above the worth of their holdings.*

IV.   *Drinking past emberfall is to be done on deck, and drunkenness will not be tolerated; transgressions to this effect will be delivered at the Captain's digression.*

V.   *All of the Company to keep their garments washed, and cutlass clean and fit for service.*

VI.   To desert the ship or quarters in time of crisis or battle is punished by death or marooning.

VII.   If any woman shall steal anything in the Company equal to the Value of a Piece of Eleven, she shall be marooned.

VIII.   If a woman shall smoke in the Hold without a cap to her pipe, or carry a candle lighted without a lantern, she shall suffer the punishment of 33 lashes.

IX.   Striking of another in the Company will result in lashes equal to the Captain's discretion.

X.   No woman to talk of breaking up their way of living, till each has shared one thousand pounds of gold. If, in order to this, any woman should lose a limb, or become a cripple in their service, she may be discharged honorably with a fair portion of the collected Hold.

XI.   The Captain and Quartermaster to receive two shares of a prize; the Master, Boatswain and Gunners

> one share and a half, and
> Musicians one and a quarter.
>
> XII. Any member of the company may
> be called out by fair rite for the
> betterment of the crew. If a
> majority of the Company agrees,
> the dispute shall be settled on deck
> through duel to first blood.

Marryk was placed on a wooden swing and hauled up the mainmast to the crow's nest. They had given him fresh clothes and were in the process of washing his rags. Now, he could see far across the ocean and long down the rocky coast. It was of course nowhere near as breathtaking as the sights he saw from the *evarik*, but it was still beautiful. Laeryn lashed him as best she could, propped up against the mast, sitting atop a barrel.

"Yer wonderin' why, aren't ya?" he asked just to break the silence.

Laeryn didn't respond.

Aera. "Why I'm still alive?"

Silence.

Marryk wasn't sure what Dyn had told them, so he had to be careful to keep their stories straight. All he could do was press: "What'd the boy say?" he decided to start.

Laeryn finally looked at him. "Said you were also picked up by the holy one. His ship was drowned, but you had the raft."

"'Ad mates once, too." *If I leave Dyn out of it, I can just tell the truth – easier that way.* He could see the urge in her throat, wanting to ask, "Go ahead."

"Fine." These piresses had no patience. "How did it happen?" she spat. However, before he could answer, she went on a little tirade, "I just don't get it. You're useless. Useless! Why would anyone keep you alive? Why do you even want to be alive? gods! I would have found a way to fling myself into the ocean—"

"And without the use'a arms and legs," he interrupted, "Ya'd drown. Don't think I 'aven't thought it." And he had, many times. But, something else told him not to. He knew he was a burden to his captain, but it was a burden Dyn had made perfectly clear he wanted to carry. Marryk kept telling himself there was a reason for this horrid thing that happened to him, and he trusted his captain – absolutely. "It 'appened," he went back to the question at hand, "'Cause I'd a run in with another Elvar, one who wasn't so curious as yer 'oliness down there. M'crew made a mistake. Thought we could steal from 'em. We were wrong. They can be silent as Shadows, ya know. And then, ya don't even realize it," he faked tears. *Or are they real?* "Crew didn't – they died. My cap'n dragged me outta there, unwillin' to leave me behind, escaped, but yer rocks back 'ere got him, killed 'im, and I was all that was left, tied to the raft. The Elvar appeared out of the mist. And the boy..." He trailed off, because if Dyr gave them an order to his alibi, he couldn't say who came first. "We still don't truly know what's gonna happen. But, I can tell ya this. We believe. By the gods, we believe. So should you when the time comes."

Laeryn looked out to the setting sun. "I would give anything to be back out there."

"Pillagin', plunderin', aye. That's the life."

"No. No, we..."

"What?"

"When we were set upon by the Fire-Guzzler, we were carrying refugees from some war we knew nothing about. Knew not where they came from. When we came upon their ship, it was floundering, and we decided to save them. Women. Children. A few old men. They had nothing, but their lives. Then and there, we decided to change our ways. We'd be mercenaries for causes we found just. So, we spared them."

"Are they still 'ere?"

She looked back at Marryk, stone-cold eyes holding back her own tears. "They were the first fed to Skyra."

"That's a quick change'a heart."

"Our captain is also our queen. She decided what we'd done had brought this mess to us. That Dûnkrath himself was offended that we were no longer slaving for war, but peace. She's never been a superstitious woman, but when you have a choice, you can choose to save. When you don't, you sacrifice. And make excuses. I hope the great Elvar will show us the way. I pray to the gods each day for release of this reef, that bargain; all I know is we're damned ... damned for something, but I refuse to believe it was for saving those people."

The sun reached its final moments of flame.

The door unlocked, and Dyn quickly returned the documents. Laeryn appeared, "His holiness requests you lead him ashore, to be his ... robe-bearer."

Dyn knew Eken made up the term to get him out of the hold. The reading was upon them, and they needed to talk. They met on the weather deck, and took the gangplank down to the rocky shore. "Did ya get anythin'?" Dyn asked. They would stay within line of sight, but were now well out of earshot of the piresses if they whispered.

"This captain-queen is cautious. She sees me as the rest of your people do, but her eyes tell me she will not give in so easily."

"Fair 'nough. She's the cap'n, and that's all there is to it. Will the stars really guide our hand? Or am I s'pposed to come up with somethin' while yer doin' ... ya know, yer thing? Yer granddaughter, Evendir—"

"I know her name."

Dyn sighed, it still hurt: *Thank the gods.* "She read fer Marryk and I from that precipice of yers – the *evarik* – and it made me a believer." He thought back, and spoke clearer: "A believer that your people were truly . . unique. That you had abilities unlike any I'd ever known. It showed us wonder, opened our eyes, to reveal us a world we'd never seen before. Maybe it was the view, maybe it was what she said, but one thing was certain – whatever she saw, the part she wouldn't talk about, also put a fear in your granddaughter's eyes."

"Reading the *evari* is a dangerous thing, Captain Kaird. The future of Aegis is not something even She can foretell. So, it is Her gift to us, some of us, to see it in the stars. Unfortunately, interpreting them is far harder than you may think. It is like finding and pulling strands of spider's silk from a web the size of a mountain. My granddaughter was very gifted ... at understanding."

"And you hanged her for it." *It should still hurt.* "For the same transgression that you're about to commit – reading to your lessers." Dyn wasn't sure why it was still such a sore spot for him. This Elvar had repented, but was that to mean forgiveness?

"The irony is not lost on me." They reached the shoreline, the sun was gone, night had fallen, and they paused. "Nor is the grief. We all make mistakes, large and small, but we must go on, even if it is the grave itself we fall into. I can only hope the future holds redemption for me. The innocent should never suffer. That was my final judgement when I led you out of our mountains the other day."

Dyn respected him for this, knowing that all could make mistakes, that everyone had flaws, and he owned up to them. He'd recognized the Elvar edicts were wrong. The sea washed over the rocks, and his feet, bringing Dyn back to their predicament.

The rest of the crew, including Marryk in the nest, watched from the carrack. Both men of the *Bighter's Wrath* wondered the same thing: Without the stone platform meticulously cut to perfection upon what the Elvar called the *evarik,* how was Ekendör Ko Ûroshyr to read the *evari.*

Ekendör removed his robe and handed it to Dyn, who played his part. He knew Marryk watched with the same fluttersparks in his stomach. Dark clouds passed over the moons when the Elvar waded into the water. Every step had purpose, his pace with meaning. Dyn could almost feel the tension washing over the deck of the *Wiles*.

When the clouds broke, and moonslight struck water, Eken glowed – literally. His figure beneath the water shone bright and clear through its crystal. It was another wonder of the ancient race no one knew about, and Dyn quickly figured out the phenomenon, though that made it no less impressive: The Elvar, or at least some of them, were tattooed with the same invisible ink they wrote their sacred texts with, that which only was illuminated underwater by moonslight. Dyn couldn't read the letters of ancient El'arria, but he recognized the designs fed through them – constellations. It was as if the entire *Evar'tûm* was etched into Eken's skin. The gasp that resonated from the *Wiles* confirmed they were no less in awe of the sight.

Eken craned his foot-and-a-half long neck up to the sky, and ran his fingers through the jet-black hair that floated about him; its graying strands of silver shimmered as weaves of fate in the gentle tide. He stayed perfectly still, even when a hungry bellow bolstered from the mountains. Unstartled, he refused to move a muscle, unwilling to disturb the water.

"She wants to be fed," the red from the rigging said in the silence that followed. Somehow, eerily, it carried down to Dyn's ears.

"Sh!" another quipped.

"There's no reason not to throw the lame to her; there's no worth to his life as it is."

"Silence, bosun," this was Laeryn.

Dyn prayed Eken was doing more than just stalling for time, that these stars were actually giving them guidance. He needed to believe in something, now, something he would never understand. And there were no plans dawning on him as he waited.

Ekendör collapsed, as if released by some unearthly pull; Dyn fought the urge to go to his side. When the Elvar resurfaced, he pulled his hair back and retied it.

They made their way back to the carrack together. "Did you... Did it..." Dyn wasn't sure how or what to ask.

"You are going to have to trust me. And I am going to have to trust you. You have a gut pirate, one that's honorable, do not let that go – for anything."

"What happened?"

Eken sighed, frustrated, "Aegis does not want this creature harmed, but does not approve of the beast's deal with them either. In Aegis' eyes, these women are a blight, while the monster is just a pain; however, the *evari* tell me something very different."

"You mean earth and star don't agree? Is that ... I mean ... how does that work?"

"This is your ödyssey, Captain Kaird. Your journey home. It is far from over, but I tell you now you will see the Ember Cities again ... if you can bear losing many more along the way under your command—"

"My command?!"

"Do you know its origins, captain?"

"Sorry, what?"

"The word – ödyssey."

"Not the way you pronounce it, but I know what it means."

"It's actually an Elvar word that's found its way into other tongues and tales. Long ago, one of our smartest Generals, Ödyssyrû So Ûrowyr, lost a great battle in our expansion Eastward across the Frostcrags; this was long before the Barrens were as such, and even longer before your Ildûron was founded. Ödyssyrû was defeated, and all that remained was a single legion of Elvar. Instead of pushing on, instead of sending for aid, he looked his soldiers in the eye, and saw the reflection within – families, wives, children, waiting for them back home. He decided he was through with war, they'd sacrificed enough, and whatever punishment lay in wait for him he would accept solely. His Elvar followed his order – absolutely. He would be tried for desertion, for treason, and take all responsibility for his men ... if they ever made it home alive. He and his legion spent years trying to get back to civilization, and when they finally reached the mountains of their home, the Elvar had all but forgotten the war. The expansion itself was recalled long before, and no one had ever sent word to Ödyssyrû. The Elvar councils couldn't admit to this, so they tried him anyway, and he was found guilty. However, his men were freed, and they found their families warm and welcoming. They had not forgotten their husbands and fathers, and were more than happy to remove the burial stones from their grounds."

"What happened to Ödyssyrû?" he pronounced the 'ö' correctly that time.

"On his way to execution, instead of walking to the gallows, Ödyssyrû leapt from the mountain's edge, and was taken by the sea. We believe he rose to the stars three days later, as his body was never found. He is one of the constellations, now."

Dyn couldn't think of what to say.

"You will need to prove yourself, like he did, to all – man, beast, earth, and sky – before you are allowed to return home, Captain Kaird."

They walked up the gangplank and onto the weather deck. Before Eken could say anything, Dyn couldn't help himself – he pointed a bold finger at the red on the rigging, "If ya even think'a throwin' me mate to that creature again, I'll make certain me master here never helps ya off this reef."

A roar cascaded down the mountain, rolling over the deck and rippling the planks.

Ekendör donned his robe, snapping it around him. "The *evari* are clear this night. You will be free of Skyra's clutches by morning." There was a cheer, until he raised his hand – silence. "However, you must sacrifice to her the one who struck this bargain, unlawful via the judgement of Aegis."

A murmur ran through the crew. Dyn was just as surprised. Did the Elvar not know? *The crew will never sacrifice their captain, even if it means disobeying a being they think of as omnipotent. Then again ... they've been stuck here for five years, and they're desperate. Is this the stars, or you, or a bloody gambit, my friend?*

"Your holiness," Laeryn spoke up, "We do not expect you to understand the ways of your lessers, so we explain respectfully: You ask the impossible. This crew is loyal."

"The stars have spoken."

"The stars do not speak for my ship," the captain-queen finally appeared from her cabin, slamming her door with finality. Apparently, she did not feel it was necessary to attend the reading. This was dangerous – she wasn't a believer.

Dyn knew it was his turn, "I challenge ya, then! If yer a Bayman true, then I challenge you in 'ccordance with pirate law, the same law set down by the Ember Kings a thousand years ago. Ya may not answer to Ildûron out 'ere, but d'ya still answer to the sea?"

The piress queen stepped up to him, and looked down. She was taller than he. "By what right, or what law do you refer to, boy?"

Dyn held his head high, "Article twelve in yer law, much like Article twelve of the great Homaeryn's law, or Article seven'a Sir Dynyk's, or … is it Article one of ol' Cap'n Byrbor's *Wrath*, I believe?"

She narrowed her eyes; she knew the law, but wondered how Dyn could know of so many versions of it. He was also slipping into a much clearer tone in his confidence…

"Yer code states: Any member of the company may be called out by fair rite for the betterment of the crew. Ya never called me 'prisoner'; therefore, I have the same right as anyone here."

She was caught. She never did. It was a mistake. They'd become so lax over the years, they didn't think about the fact that anyone aboard not taken prisoner, was simply added to the Company. Again, even if it wasn't pirate law, it was pirate common courtesy. "And what betterment do you speak of?"

"Freedom, I think, is better than being beached, is it not?!" he called out to the crew, whose nerves kept them quiet, but Dyn saw the rise in their beating hearts, bounding for conflict. "I believe the reading of mine own savior."

"The terms?" she knew she'd lost – the crew was sick of it all, and would hold onto any hope offered to leave.

"I leave that to yer holiness," Dyn turned, "Please, great one, I wish to serve, and thus I have, now. What is it you'd see done."

"This accord is barbaric." The Elvar walked the deck, feigning to think. "But if it is to serve Aegis, and follow Her will, I will see it through. Do your dance, whatever it may be. If my servant wins, we adhere to the reading. If my servant loses, may his body serve instead the will of the stars."

The mutiny would come if she refused, "Agreed. Bring the blades, quartermaster."

The blades were simple knives, no longer than a forearm, and as a cabin boy for much of his life, Dyn had very little training; he hoped the years spent wrecked here had dulled the captain-queen's talent. If not, he didn't have a chance. The outcomes raced through his mind: *What will I do if I lose? What's the plan? Oh gods, I'll be eaten.*

Their hands were bound, and he was forced to use his off-hand as he'd been the accuser. Their dance didn't take them far about the deck, encircled as they were by the piresses; it was mostly rough thrusting techniques and swiping maneuvers. Neither was allowed to strike each other's bound arm, but the captain-queen proved deft, and the flexibility in her shoulders astounding. In the end, she whirled beneath both their arms to come around on his offside, and Dyn felt her iron dig into his arm – a subtle, but sharp pain, far more precise than it should have been. She'd done this before. And she shoved him to his knees.

Dyn looked up at Eken, ready to say goodbye, but the Elvar just mouthed: *Trust me.*

Oh for 'zhri's sake, Dyn thought, *he knew I'd lose.*

The next strike cut the rope that held them together.

"We take him to the beast!" the captain-queen cried out, and the roar of her mates followed.

When she looked to Ekendör, he simply nodded, serene as ever.

"I will go with you, to see that Aegis is satisfied."

As they made ready to depart, Dyn whispered to Ekendör, "You knew I'd lose."

"Of course."

"Alright, 'fore we gotta hide that we're friends again, if that's what we are, sir, do you really know this thing, this monster?"

Ekendör chuckled (the first time anyone, outside the *Evar-aeor*, in history might have heard an Elvar do this): "Actually, yes."

"Really? What is it?"

Ekendör scanned the carrack to make certain everyone was still busy, "You must understand that not all creatures of Aegis were a blessing. She made mistakes, too. Accidents happen during all creation ... large and small. The Elvar believe Skyra is one of them. We have avoided her for centuries. She would find our caverns and halls, and prey on our people; we warred with her for decades before we couldn't take any more death. The entire Eastern Sanctuary is abandoned, for our fear of her return. However, of late, we've seen little of her – now, we know why."

"Right. Why bother hunting for it, when food can be brought to yer doorstep."

There were seven of them in all that went ashore – the captain-queen, Laeryn the quartermaster, two gunners, a boatswain, Dyn and Ekendör.

The quartermaster oversaw Dyn, and pushed him forward. It wasn't long before the party was parted, paces away from each other, as the rocks made the walk treacherously difficult, a labyrinth of sorts. "Why'd you keep that other man alive after taking his raft?" Laeryn needed to know. "If he has no use of his arms or legs, what good is he?"

"Curious, are we?"

"I just don't understand."

"His mind's still sharp, which I can say is more than yer lunatic feeding innocents to this monster can say for herself."

Silence.

Something is wrong. "Ya don't agree with her, do you?"

"We follow our captain and queen."

This was a voice of pride, not loyalty. Dyn had heard it before, it was always the voice used before Byrbor broke their prisoners, and turned them into traitors.

The captain appeared in front of them, startling them, "Have you seen Nyrna?"

"No, sir, we've been following you as best we can. Can't see much else around these boulders."

"She was between us, now lost."

Eken appeared high on a rock, an ominous silhouette against the sun, "Maybe the beast is closer than you think, and hungrier."

They continued without finding the missing girl, but Dyn knew it was Eken. His first encounter with the Elvar began similarly – people dying in the Shadows. It appeared all Elvar were trained this way.

A few dozen feet on, and the captain-queen was once more out of earshot. "He's also m'friend," Dyn shrugged, backtracking to her previous curiosity.

"Didn't you just meet?"

"It was a fast kindlin' of friendship. Related a lot. Bein' almost drowned 'n all."

"... How noble."

"Maybe. Or maybe I just don't believe anyone should be left behind."

She sighed, *the first sign of breaking*, "We were like you, once. This reef changed her. Broke our morals as much as our ship."

"It may've broken yer cap'n, made her bargain with the unnatural, but that don't mean ya have to play along."

"This is not a game. We are only alive because of her."

"Some of you ... are only alive, that is." He'd had a brief moment with Marryk before they'd departed – he knew their tragic means, the truth of their sacrifices.

"It is what it is."

"And if somethin' changed?"

Silence.

That was all he needed.

A second piress disappeared, and Dyn saw the fury rising in the captain-queen's face, flushed. She must have known it was Eken. Once more, he appeared, and said, "How big is this beast? She's a sly fellow, is she?"

The captain-queen said nothing but, "Walk with me Elvar, I would ask to be graced by your presence for the remaining trek."

She would watch him, because she couldn't be outnumbered. There were still three piresses to Eken and Dyn.

The moons were high when Dyn began to see signs of structures, outlines of homes once in residence across the coast; he could only imagine how far the Elvar Realm stretched before Skyra began her hunt. "Do you know how far it is?" he asked Laeryn. "I know I'm bein' sacrificed 'n all, but by the gods my legs are gettin' tired."

"She usually takes them alone. Most are not as healthy as you, or dangerous. And she doesn't trust the Elvar."

"Neither did I. But... Oh, Laeryn, I've seen wondrous things,' he finally used her name to strike at her heart. "What a great show this'll be for ya though, right? My blood's gonna go everywhere, I hope ya like stains to that leather—"

"Stop it."

"Piress, when I was a cap'n, this muck wouldn't be tolerated. The first Article, ya know. What's yers?"

"You already know the answer to that."

"Yeah? When ya decide to follow yer own crew's creed, let me know ... if I ain't already dead. Your captain-queen," he articulated and spat, "Is following her own."

Somehow, the third piress of the party disappeared before they reached their destination, leaving Laeryn, the captain-queen, Eken, and Dyn.

The offering spot was no different than Dyn expected – the opening to a massive cave. It had the remains of persons and animals, bones and feces scattered all about. "Chain him down," the captain-queen ordered. He could tell she was nervous.

Laeryn kicked Dyn to his knees and shackled him to fetters waiting for the lamb. They had been secured to the rocks long before, and here the terrain was well worn by the monster claiming its meals; snapped harpoons and rusted swords littered the skeletal terrain. The quartermaster paused at the final manacle.

"Ya don't have to do this," Dyn pled quickly, quietly, one last time.

"Whilst she lives, I follow no other."

"What the Elvar read in the stars cannot be wrong, you have to trust him."

"If he is right, it will be shown, and Aegis herself will free you."

Dyn wasn't about to wait for Aegis, so when she moved back to her captain-queen, he immediately shifted his body to check the fetters. They were wrought-iron, with what looked to be a simple lock. Unfortunately, if he tried to pick it, they would see.

This was not lost on Eken, who moved slowly into position, his robes falling over the area where the manacles were secured, and body hiding Dyn's efforts from piress view.

The captain-queen shouted, "Oh mighty Skyra, I bring you this offering in trade for our lives!"

Here, the roar did not just tremble the earth, it split cracks in a few rocks as well. The residual aftershock, Dyn realized, was his heart beating with dread and fear, and by that time, the thing lurched from the cave. At first, all that whipped out was a slithering tentacle, squid-like in nature. Dyn recognized it, as Byrbor had taken a full year to hunt one between wars. He'd seen every sketch and rendering of these creatures, studied them in grave detail with his captain, fascinated at the prospect of eating one (it was quite good, in the end). This time, it terrified him. At least twice as large, the tentacle's manus wrapped around the captain-queen, while the dactylus end smacked Laeryn back to a boulder, where she landed hard and stayed frozen. A hundred little suckers suctioned one by one across the captain-queen's body, molesting her, popping on and off, squeezing tighter and tighter, but she never cried out – this was how she sacrificed them all. Then, from the depths of the cave appeared the rest of her, this creature called Skyra.

Instead of a squid-like head, it funneled into the body of something else entirely. *Is it a woman?* Dyn thought, petrified himself. *The body, the breasts, the arms, are like that of the strongest piress...*

But then, he saw the neck. It reminded him of the Elvar, milky white and ribbed, but far more snake-like. It was at least five feet long, and curved and coiled side to side, forward and back, a serpent from shoulder to jaw. *It's jaw!* It snapped, three layers of teeth, he saw, far sharper than any predator of the sea or blade of the mountain, and Skyra clicked her tongue, lapping out of its maw somewhere between that of a rabid dog's lolling and witting snake's hissing.

The captain-queen struggled one arm to freedom, and pointed at Dyn; however, Skyra saw Ekendör first.

He'd moved gracefully away to a nearby boulder, and now stood atop it, no longer needing to crane his neck to confront the beast eye to eye. As a race, the Elvar did not deign to look up to anything but the stars, and neither was Eken different from them, nor this monstrosity different than who he saw as his lessers.

Ekendör spoke soft and slow, but it carried, and Skyra heard him clearly, "Skyrakûrzhri, your pact with this lowly thing is unbefitting your ancient line. Aegis has spoken to me through starlight and moonstide, and She is displeased with your actions. Be done with these fools, this pettiness, this lazy whim, and return to the mountains," he paused, "Or Aegis will have to make a choice. It is a choice She has made before."

Skyra hissed and snapped. While Dyn knew nothing about monsters, he knew how a snake struck, and he saw it coming. Surely, Eken knew as well, but still hadn't moved. *Why isn't he moving?!*

Dyn finished picking the lock hastily, slipped from the fetters, and darted to the nearest skeleton. He snatched up a harpoon from the deceased, and leapt from rock to rock, crag to boulder, watching the creature reel back its neck. When it shot forward, Dyn was there. He leapt in front of Eken and braced the butt of the harpoon against the rock. It speared the roof of Skyra's mouth, and she immediately sprung back.

Dyn flipped the harpoon over in his hand to throw, but stayed his hand with patience. Skyra was taking a second look around.

Furious, the monster shook her head, and tightened her grip around the captain-queen. The woman struggled frantically, "No-no-no! We had a bargain!"

Ekendör boomed down to her, "The Ildra do not bargain with their lessers." Dyn could only imagine what the Elvar looked like, standing tall and powerful against the stormy sky. He was the last thing the woman saw, as Skyra snapped her spine and carried her into the mountain. A hissing voice echoed back on the wind, but Dyn couldn't say if it was the dying breath of the captain-queen, some magical voice of this monster, or the mountain itself, "Your time will come, Elvar. You are all doomed."

Dyn dropped to his shins, adrenaline draining from his body, muscles shaking uncontrollably. This low, Eken was revealed as well: Though the Elvar hadn't moved an inch, his legs trembled ever so lightly, betraying his fear, and relief thereof. Dyn's gaze fell to Laeryn, who simply sat in awe below them.

"We have proved one thing today," Eken said.

"The gods are with us?" Dyn asked.

Eken rose a brow.

"The stars are with us?" Dyn tried again.

Eken cocked his head down.

"You people aren't just crocks?"

Eken smiled, "That you are a captain worth following. Never abuse this trust."

Dyn found the strength to stand again, "A'right, well, so ... what did – whatever that was – mean? About yer ... your people?"

Ekendör looked back to the cave, "I don't know. But it is not the first time I have been warned."

Dyn thought for a moment. *Evendir.* "Your granddaughter?"

"Was hung for the same, and we called it heresy. We did not listen then. We would not listen now. If I ever make it home, maybe they will listen before it is too late."

"Well, m'friend, if we ever make it home – to my home – yer more'en welcome to stay with me." Dyn smiled, but saw the sorrow in Eken's eyes. He was worried, and had every right to be so.

It didn't take much. Dyn was anointed captain with leave of the quartermaster, as Laeryn was more than happy to follow him, now, and the rest of the crew fell in line when they were told the tale. By the time they broke free of the reef, everyone considered their voyage blessed by the stars. Captain Dyn Kaird was their savior; Ekendör Ko Ûroshyr was their prophet; and Marryk ... was just Marryk, but the best crow they'd ever had.

Dyn made a point to learn all their names immediately: Maera, the red from the rigging, took quite fondly to Marryk quite fast; Sita was the only gunner left alive; and the twins Dyta and Dötyr were boatswains he'd never be able to tell apart.

When they hit open water, the sun was bright, and the skies were clear.

An Evendain's Existence

High Lord Zain-evare Fyrön

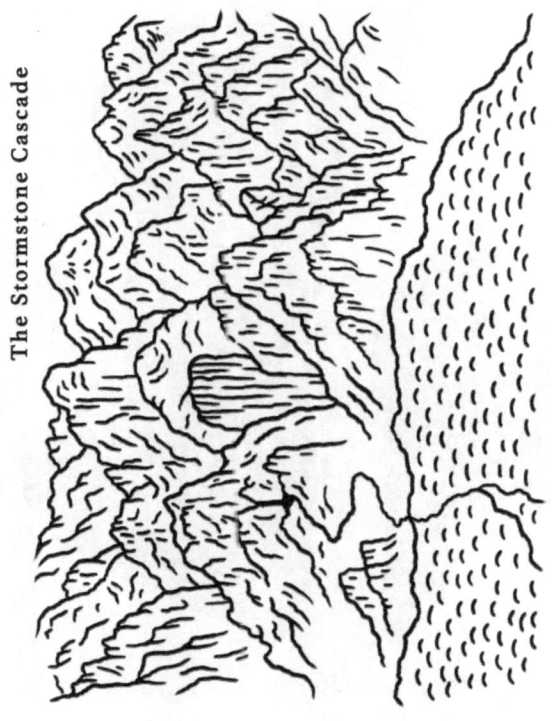

The Stormstone Cascade

...being a short story during the Age of Origin, approximately in the year 819...

Zain-evare Fyrön abandoned Galaborne, the self-righteous knight-errant of Nûmundor bent on his holy crusade, in the citadel, now far behind him. Fyrön took the Cascade's *raeordûmn* from its place on the promenade for himself, and he travelled long to return home with the Heartstone of his people. Through the twisting tunnels of the deep and dark Stormstones he walked, slow and sure through the Worldvein, and thought long and hard on the future – not something the Evendain were known to do. What Galaborne said in the library weighed heavy on his mind, and made Fyrön question all he understood as purpose.

Inclined as he was to take the stone to his people, that they could study it through the eyes of wise council, he did no such thing upon his return home. The desire to analyze it alone, to learn all he could of its mysticism himself, was too strong. Where the stones came from and what purpose they had as the so-called 'Hearts' of the Realms could be the most profound discovery of their time, and it could change what his people knew to be true about Aegis.

A strange whisper called to him, bade him sit in the Shadow of his personal quarter. Thus, he obeyed, sitting on a bench at the foot of his bed. As High Lord, he was one of six who received privacy in such. However, now, in the tightening moments between betrayal and knowledge, the six walls that fashioned the room a hexagon never felt so close.

He stared at the stone, drawn into its obfuscation. Stealing it away from its holy altar was a crime, but all that transpired in the tower made him question the very existence of the Evendain as a people. Should he share this doubt, much ill could come of it – denial at least, reformation at worst. If it held some revelation, he was unsure if he'd even wish to share it. If the truth lay deeper than the Beginning as they knew it, he feared the knowledge. And while he was wary of his own greed creeping up his intent, rising from the moment he took the thing, he dreaded its secrets more. He needed to know, "What will you do to our people, I wonder?"

Free them.

It was a susurration, no matter its eeriness, that kindled his curiosity and damned him in the end. Whatever consequence may befall him, he knew he could take responsibility for it. There was only one thing left to do – take the offensive, take the plunge.

Emptiness struck him the moment his fingers graced the Heartstone's surface – smooth, cold, sharp – then, burning – love's lost desire? Throes of torment washed over him, and he bastioned himself against them. Natural despair pierced his heart, but he fought the volley and cut the shafts down. The clarion abyss engulfed him, and he dove willingly into its unknown with purpose driving his mind. He would know the stone's. His second hand dropped to the bench and gripped tight to secure his tie to reality. "Your chasms of nothing shall not overwhelm me, stone of storm, stone of lightning and Shadow; I conquer you!" Fyrön felt its attempts to dominate his mind, to rip volition from thought to servitude, "I serve Aegis, not you!"

He heard its thought ring clear in his head, now, echoing between his ears like a drum and sparking his nerves to conflict:

Why?

Fyrön wasn't surprised when it answered. "You are truly alive, then, and I can speak to you?"

If using your mouth comforts you.

"I need to know my words are my own. What are you?"

A question, as it is, complicated. Power.

"Power?"

To give. To take.

"Power is to be untrusted—"

Controlled.

"We are controlled by Her."

Are you?

"We are but Her servants, the first of the Twelve, and wear our collars proudly."

Why?

"You ask this again? I say it is who we are, and always have been."

Dare you not to seek freedom?

"We know not the taste of it, so no desire to. It is a stranger to me."

Fear, then.

"If it must be called so, yes. Can I change this? No."

Yes.

This unsettled Fyrön. Was this not what drove his intent? He needed to know, but didn't want to ask.

You think you know what you are? Dare you to know the truth?

The truth was passed down for centuries. Their histories were laid out in mosaics in the halls of their home so all would remember. It was not wrong.

From a certain point of view.

"Show me," the words finally released like a prisoner behind the bars of his lips. The orb sparked and split, and it was as if he was caught within the crystalline shell. Images of the Evendain from centuries past flashed before his eyes, or his mind's eye as it were. A hundred pairs of eyes opened – their birth beneath the Cascade. He saw hands, all bone and sinew, use pick and axe to open the Worldvein, a deep and secret passage. Its purpose was lost to them in history, but it was their purpose in the Beginning to stretch it far and wide. He knew this, at least, was a fact.

As you say.

Fyrön saw the same hands seeding the great forest south of the mountains, to hide a place called by them the Shadowgourge, yet again they'd forgotten why. The Ildraeor came, as was the old way, and reshaped the land under the fires of their great maws. Evendain died by the dozen; still, She commanded their work to continue. He saw them plant the beds of flowers that blossomed across the Highlands to the north, and saw them mine the minerals of Her core. They seeded Aegis, and She fed them. They nurtured Her, and She bathed them in riches. But, all the while, it was as if they were in search of something they'd never found. So much of what the Evendain were and did was never given a reason why.

"Because we never had to question Her will."

And if you did?

"We obey. It is our purpose for being."

His vision ignited – the first war between the Evendain and the Fyrzhor over six hundred years ago.

You protect what you don't understand.

"Yes," he answered, "For Her. You. We protect the likes of you."

No! We are not Her! You obey the weak, the fragile. You protect all we pity, a Vein poisoned with mercy and drowned in love. But, you'll fail. You'll fail, and only scars and Shards will remain.

It was losing patience, and Fyrön still didn't know the answer, "What are you, and what do you want?"

Escape. From your chains. Fetters of failure and false faith. With us by your side, you will no longer feel Her pull on your mind and body, Her ceaseless need for your hand. You will be free, and your people will be yours

Another vision flashed before Fyrön's eyes.

The High Lord stood aboveground, looking out across the Cascade from a great stronghold. He felt the whole of the world at his command, even the lightning harnessed around his Shadow and struck where he favored. Fyrön walked down the spires of the stronghold, crooked and stained. He reached the foothills and crouched, touched his hand to Aegis' flesh, and She was at his force of will – he was all-powerful. He could lead the world into a new age, in which the Evendain need not dwell beneath the mountain Shadow, but rise up as Kings, masters to all below them. They would never need look down in servitude or up in dream again. The world would be theirs ... his.

Fyrön smiled. Whatever these seeing stones were, they could change the face of Aegis forever.

Yes.

"No."

No?

"I deny you. For now. The existence of the Evendain will change, but I am patient, and it will be I who decide when to break our chain."

Very well, slave. Very well.

An Reignman's Return

Nûmiel, River-Daughter

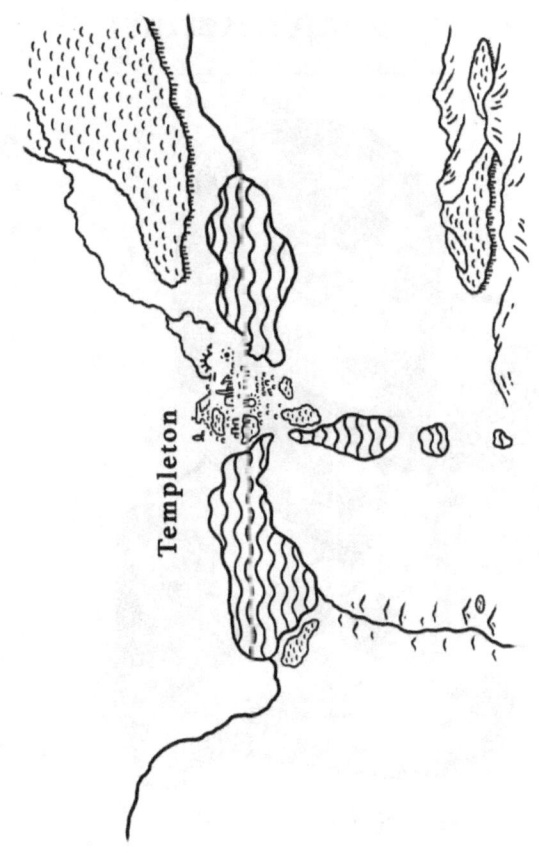

...being a short story during the Age of Origin,
approximately in the year 828...

Nûmiel dipped the cloth into the water bucket, and pressed it against her father's forehead. She braced herself for another coughing fit, but it didn't come. However, he muttered and mumbled of an angel among devils, a story he'd told for thirteen years to anyone who'd listen. When her father returned from the *Lûle'vitûm*, she was six, and understood very little of his fantastic story, but a part of him had always remained beneath the glittering canopies of the daemonwood. It wasn't long before the people had coined him for 'Crazy Ol' Nûrian,' or the 'Loon at the Loom,' as he had taken quietly to weaving when he was no longer welcome on the river. Nûmiel wondered if she'd find herself on that river, as he had, venturing into the unknown, as her father would be taking a very different river, soon, unto Shadow.

The cloth did nothing to soothe him – consumption was not a curable disease. She wondered if there was anything at all that could ease his suffering...

She left the Healer's House at midday, and entered the Western apothecary. The matron at the counter was busy with a robust customer in finery beyond the common folk of Templeton, so Nûmiel waited as patiently as she could manage. Her father could die any moment. That thought put her foot to tapping, and her foot tapping brought the patron around, irritated:

"We're in the middle of something here, woman. Come back later."

Seeing him from the front, Nûmiel knew exactly who he was – they all did. Baron Ticzûr was the profound pig of the noble class that ruled over them, and not to be trifled with. She had to be very careful what she said, or she'd be in more trouble than her father. "Lord, my apologies, sincerely, but I may not."

His eyes flashed, "Excuse me?!"

"My father," she said quickly, "My father is ill, and I need to find something to soothe him this night, pray he makes it to morning."

"What ails him, miss?" the matron cut in.

"Consumption—"

"Ha!" Ticzûr guffawed, "He may as well take his leave now, 'en. M'cousin died of that two years past, and we'd brought medicines from across the Spine of the bloody World to save him. There's nothing this old hag can do for you. Get out." He waved her off.

Nûmiel hesitated, but the matron shook her head, and added quietly, "I'm sorry, but the Baron is correct."

"Of course, I am!"

"Nûrian, right?"

Nûmiel nodded.

Ticzûr grabbed his gut, as if it hurt to laugh, "The coot who talks of the devils in the dark? The man who dared the daemonwood and went mad? It'll be good to rid the streets of him."

Nûmiel's grip tightened, and she felt her nails prick into her palms where her fist clenched.

"I said. Get out," Ticzûr repeated coldly.

Nûmiel held her tongue, and didn't dare address the matron again, whose eyes filled with pity – like that could do her any good. Therefore, she bowed respectfully, and turned to leave.

As she did, the Baron called back a statement of finality to push her on her way, "The *rhignsör* is all he needs now, river-daughter."

It was odd that he used the term river-daughter; it wasn't one of hostility, but respect for those of the river-trade that ran the Reignway. Her father hadn't done so in years, and it was a name she'd nigh forgotten she bore. Regardless, the man of power was right – there wasn't anything she, or anyone else, could do, now.

The *rhignsör* was a coin of sorts, a morbidly specific one placed on the forehead of the dead. It was meant to pay the ferryman to take them down the *dain'rhil*. The haunting, cowled boatman, Syrghas, weighed the payment against a life's worth, and the reeds of the river of death would part, split to the Riverborne and the Riverwraith. One ferried the dead unto Shadow, the other into Spirit, a test of both in passing.

Rhignsör itself, also known as water-silver, was a rare metal even apothecaries did not carry – it was a bad omen, because of its higher purpose; however, alchemists were rumored to use it for other, unholy, tricks as well. Just handling the coin was blasphemy in Templeton, even treated properly. After funerals, the loved-one who handled it would immediately take to confession with the Priests of the Second.

Because of this, *rhignsör* could only be found one place legally – the Burial House, and the cost would be high...

Calling it the Burial House was a misnomer, and confusing to outsiders, because there were absolutely no burials in Templeton. Reignmen did not bury their dead – they laid them in a boat, lain with the colors of their state, and cast the boat downriver where it met the sea. At sea, and at a time of his choosing, the ferryman would pull the boat under, and greet them on the banks of the *dain'rhil*. This ceremony was one of many that caused so much strife between the 'Hearth and the Embers. The Baymen believed in the water as well, moreso even, as much of their lives were spent at sea; however, they desecrated the spirits of their dead by forging coffins, laden heavy and sealed with their worldly possessions, to sink. In the bed of the reefs they would lie forever; Nûmiel knew little else of the tradition, but was sure it couldn't get much worse.

As it was, the Burial House was, in truth, a shipyard, albeit a small one, where the boats of the passed were fashioned for the dead. The man running the yard was also the man who dealt in the *rhignsör*.

She entered the House for no other reason than anyone else, so Malson the Master did not greet her any differently than the rest, "Crazy Nûrian dead, then?"

"He's not—," she caught herself. There was no time to defend a man who would still die infamously a nut. "No, but ... I need to be prepared for such. The silver..."

"Three silvers for water-silver, my dear."

She wasn't surprised, but her heart sank. "Please, I have maybe a tenth of that."

"The river costs."

"Please, sir, I will pay you back, I promise. I need it before—"

"He passes, aye." The sinewy man leaned forward, "Or he'll roam forever the banks of the *'ghis*. But, before he pays Syrghas, you pay me."

"I don't – I can't –" she stuttered.

"Then, pray to the Tenth your father's not taken in his sleep."

The self-proclaimed Master of the Dead knew she would find a way to pay him. There was, of course, always a way, and she only accepted it when she saw who was in the market.

Amongst the crowds of the bazaar, Baron Ticzûr himself was sifting through a vendor's gems and jewels. He had a wife, a renowned and insatiably greedy one, and the Baron's coin purse hung lightly-secured to his robes' loops. Nûmiel would never go unnoticed herself, but found her savior nearby. A little boy eyeing a fruit stand caught her attention, as she knew exactly what he was. She walked up, "Excuse me."

The boy tried to run before even turning, but Nûmiel caught his arm, whirled him about, and knelt to his level. "I need your help."

No one cared for the ruling Barony that controlled Templeton's trade and commerce guilds, but it was the price they paid for living in the greatest civilized city in all the realms. After all, they were the first and only place across all Aegis, as far as anyone was concerned, that constructed aqueducts, used sewage systems, and lit their streets at night with a series of lamps that reflected light via strategically placed mirrors.

Therefore, it didn't take long to convince the urchin to help her. He was off in a blitz, and disappeared, while Nûmiel popped up next to the Baron with a smile, "Oh, milord, it's so good to see you again."

Ticzûr stared at her, disarmed by her change of demeanor. "Continue to bother me, and you'll be appreciating my presence from the stockade."

She moved closer and batted her eyes, "I just wanted to apologize for my tone earlier; I didn't mean to waste your time."

"Of course, of course," he disregarded her, trying to move along.

"Are you troubled, milord? Could I be of any help?"

He grumbled, "Hmm. Yes, well, possibly, I suppose you might. The Baroness has made it very clear her weariness with the thousands of pieces she has, and wants something new, unique to add to her collection. She needs it now, for an event at the manor tonight. None of this looks any different to me, then what she already has, and I've paid thrice over for." He stopped here.

Nûmiel waited, knowing it was a test of the patience she lacked earlier.

She passed, and the Baron nodded, "You may give me your opinion."

Nûmiel nodded, "Thank you, milord. I believe you are not at fault, but it's this market – so dull and dreary as it is this time of year. In fact, if I may be so bold," – she pulled a ring from her own finger – "a gift. It's set with a stone my father brought back from the *Lûle'vitûm*." The lie was easy, as her father's infamy was sound. What precious stones he *had* brought back, only one was kept, and that was hidden well away from prying eyes and thieving hands. The ring that fat Ticzûr took from her now was a simple amber, but she doubted either him or his wife would notice.

Ticzûr stared at it, caught it in the sunlight to check its shine, "From the daemonwood, you say? Hmm."

"You could say, truly, there is none like it in all the city, or possibly the Realm if you wish, as no one dares venture beneath those canopies. Especially after my father ... you know..." she didn't even have to feign the sadness she felt in such reflection.

Ticzûr raised a skeptic brow, "And you're willing to part with it, an heirloom as such? I doubt this."

"I would be honored if my father's legacy was more than considered madness, even if just a small favor was done by you to honor his passing." She waited, and wondered if she could have just sold it to the Baron for the coin, but knew in her heart he'd never buy from the likes of her. Free, and placing him on a pedestal to do her this ridiculous honor, was the only way to chance the theft.

At length, the Baron agreed, took the ring, and left without so much as looking back down to the purse of coin no longer at his side. She breathed a sigh of relief; the boy was good, Nûmiel hadn't even seen him.

She prayed he'd keep his end of the deal.

He did. Meeting her outside the Burial House, the boy looked up at her, "I'm sorry about it all. I always thought his stories were funny, sure, but they made me wanna go on adventures, ya know? Thought I might see the daemons myself one day."

She smiled, "Don't be in a rush, kid, trust me."

Nûmiel paid the Master of the Dead without a word, and loathed the smile spread across lips cracked and teeth rotting.

She returned to her father in haste, but the Healer shook her head. "I'm sorry, dear. It wasn't long ago, you still have time for the rites. We'll set him off properly, if you have the payment."

Nûmiel's tears fell silently. She placed the coin on Crazy Old Nûrian's forehead. "Goodbye father. I love you."

An Eleaos'i's Devotion

Lökaeal'i, Devoted Husband

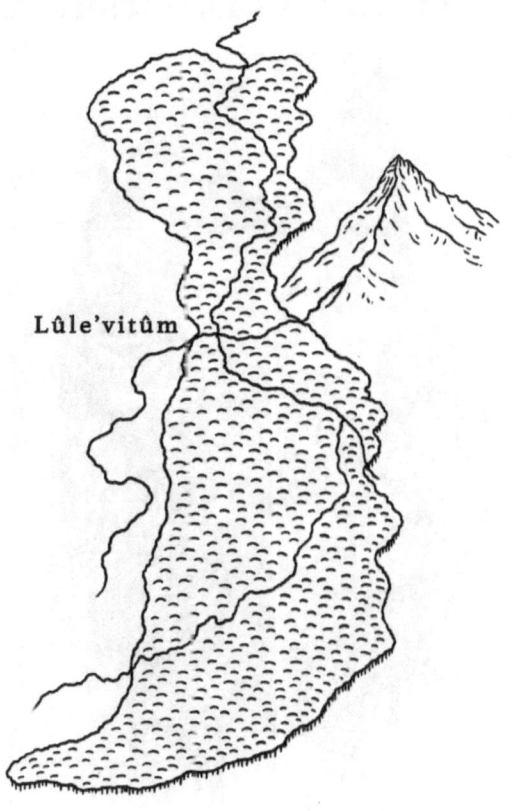

Lûle'vitûm

*...being a short story during the Age of Origin,
approximately in the year 845...*

Lökaeal'i knelt at the borders of the *Lûle'vitûm*, head titled down in reverence to the shimmering boughs, a canopy glistening in the morning sun; its leaves were thick and vibrant with the orange, red, and yellow of Ûroghas. He'd returned ... home? *No,* he thought, *Nûmundor is my home – I am a Nûmunyr, not an Eleaos'i. I am a broken limb of the Great Elm.* If there was one thing he must accept, it was this: *The Eleaos'i will not have forgotten my crime, the infraction that fractured the very whole of our ... their ... people. Even after thirty years, they will not forgive me. Would anything have changed since then, I wonder? No.* The Eleaos'i were a naturally long-lived people, the Fourth graced them with the nigh ageless life of the very Elm they were split from; unfortunately, the immortal did not grant them the gift of understanding or clemency. *You know why you are here. Do it, and be done with the place.*

Asira was dying. His wife, the love of his life, and the woman who'd accepted him as he was, *what* he was, afore all others in Nûmundor, was fading into Shadow. Now, he'd crossed the Spine of the World again, returned to the most dangerous place a traitor could be, amidst those he betrayed, to save her. Like many things in the glittering wood, a beauty found nowhere else in the realms, there was one unique bit of nature that could cure her here.

The sickness started with chest pain and minor coughing. At first, Lök thought she'd caught a bug when the Thrush-King held the Festival of the Moraintyri. This year was unconventionally overcrowded, as the man had apparently brokered a truce with his enemies. Peoples from all across the Wreatheland had gathered at this city of equality to revel in the rains and to speak of the year to come. By the time the first of Ûroghas rolled around, and the guests departed, Asira's sickness was more than a bug. Lök kept shut their doors and windows, told her not to take one step outside, and to see no one – he'd seen it before, and knew, if it spread, it could kill every man, woman, and child in Nûmundor.

Decades before, when he still lived under the leaves of the *Lûle'vitûm*, a small village, whose inhabitants called it Islör, suffered a similar epidemic that almost eradicated the population. Spread by its own coughing fits, it consumed the lungs of its prey. When a local wise-woman came to Islör, she'd studied the disease until contracting it herself. She ventured into the surrounding woodland the villagers feared, as the Eleaos'i were known as tricksters in the least, and devils at their worst. Yet, she went un-harassed by them. Lök himself was one who defended this decision by the elders in council to keep her safe, fearing the disease may spread into the wood, and inevitably them. At that time, most of the Eleaos'i were on his side, but that was a long time ago. On the verge of death, the wise-woman found the hollow of a tree that grew a moldy lichen which she devised and produced a cure with. Islör was saved.

When Lök found blood in Asira's handkerchief, he knew it was the same disease, and accepted the road ahead of him. Now, he prayed to the Fourth to hide him from his forsaken kin, and the speed to return to his beloved whilst she still lived.

Lökaeal'i waited for night to fall, then kept to the forest floor. The Eleaos'i watched, waited, prayed, and even slept in the canopies, so he slipped from shade to Shadow out of sight. There was no lack of cover; nevertheless, he kept scrutiny skyward to spot any eyes on him. When the clouds cleared, and starlight conquered the sky, everything got trickier. There were fewer paths and smaller slivers where Shadow could take him one step to the next. It wasn't long until he was forced to cross very visible paths. Not long after that, he felt their eyes upon him.

Before he fled to Nûmundor, he'd always been the predator. After that, he became just another simpleton of the city, a wood-carver and toy-maker in service to the Thrush. Now, he felt solely the prey – alone, unsafe, and in constant fear of his life. It pressed on his mind, and the trees felt like they were closing in, enemies on every limb. If he was going to survive, he needed to respect, if not become, what he used to be – Elmborne. It wasn't long before he heard the guttural clicking of the tongue he knew was a signal the Root-stalkers used when they were in position.

There was no more time.

Lök's haunches bent, and he sprung into the trees. Nûmundor had no lack of woodland, but the trees of the *Lûle'vitûm* held a special place in his heart. When his talons wrapped around the branches of the closest elm, his heart skipped a beat, and his hand went to the trunk to steady his flight. He gained his balance, stood tall, breathed in the life he'd lost, and fell backward.

He arched in his descent, nabbed the nearest limb, and swung nigh a full circle before letting go. He arced aloft, and never touched the ground again – bounding across the canopy in the moonslight.

Lök could no longer fool himself; they saw him, and he was being followed. They tracked his every leap and bound, now, well into the night. If he stopped, they would catch him. If they caught him, it was over. And he knew they were curious. Curiosity led to many visitors' deaths in the *vitûm*, but he never thought it would be his own.

When he crossed the river, he used his talons – sharpened before his travels – to snap free the vines, and cut through the branches, that intertwined the eastern bank with the western canopies. It wouldn't stop his predators, but it would stall them. Now, they would need to cross much farther north, and his destination was just a short distance south if the grove still grew tall.

It did.

He spotted the tree. It was of the *lûmae* family of flora, and Lök knew it was time for a quick, decisive plan of attack: Find the bole, enter the hollow, skim as much of the lichen as possible, then get out. He couldn't say how much time the river crossing bought him, but knew he had no time to spare.

Lök's claws pierced the tree's trunk, and he worked his way around the perimeter. When he found the hole, he peered inside. The cavity wasn't large, but he was able to slip inside as any Eleaos'i of common stature.

Within, the hollow tree was dark, so he felt around the base of the bark hastily. His heart rose when his hands ran over the damp, wooly lichen. He broke off pieces of the bark that bore the fungus, and shoved as much in his bag as would fit. The cracking echoed through the small space, masking the entrance of his enemy.

"You didn't even hear me enter, brother. I could have already killed you."

Lök whirled around to face his natural kin. "My senses may have dulled in thirty years, but what elder creature's doesn't, eh?" he said with a smile, buying time. This younger adversary was right – he was no Eleaos'i when it came to instinct anymore, but this boy in front of him was curious. *Can I convince him to stay his hand?*

"I've heard stories about you. The branch that broke the limb that cracked the tree. You betrayed your own kind."

"I had my reasons, and I do not regret them."

"We are one. But, you were you. Why?"

Lök noticed the boy had moved himself into a position to attack, and saw the hunter's knees begin to bend. *Last chance:* "I have a wife. She's dying. I returned only to retrieve that which can heal her."

In the end, this boy was not him. The hunter had no room in his heart for pleading or mercy; instead, he launched himself at his elder. Lök rolled out of the way, but shock of the ground shuddered through his shoulder into his spine painfully. Adrenaline kicked through his body, and Lök realized there was no way to beat this boy Eleaos'i to Eleaos'i. *It's a good thing I'm a Nûmunyr, now.*

The hunter charged, and Lök took the brunt of it full force. It threw the boy offguard, as it was not the way of the Elmborne – they focused on acrobatic strike and defense over brutish techniques. Thusly, Lök chose not to, he held his ground, talons digging into the earth, and found his hands on the boy's throat. He flipped his enemy to the ground, and stood over him.

"You are still my brother; I will not kill you." Lök sprang toward the opening to escape the hollow, but the boy was quicker. Talons dug into Lök's ankle on ascension, and pulled him back down. They tumbled over each other, but Lök, having wrestled many times with the guards of Nûmundor, found himself on top. Without thinking, trained in the way of the Thrushmen, he heard the boy's neck snap. When all motion ceased, and Lök realized how far his self-defense had taken him, he fell back and crawled away. *The branch that broke the limb that cracked the tree. And now, I've carved my name through its trunk in blood.*

He couldn't waste any more time. He leapt from the *lûmae* and escaped through the night. Many eyes followed him, many feet tracked him, but none caught up with him.

By dawn, he'd reached the Spine of the World, and was on his way home.

Lökaeal'i knelt at Asira's bed, and fed her the tonic, boiled with the lichen and other healing properties, slowly. It had taken some time to get all the way back to Nûmundor, but his devotion conquered his weariness.

"Did you make it back to that shimmering place? Was it still as beautiful, as wonderful, as you've told me?"

Lök gave his beloved a warm smile, "Always. Nothing ... nothing ever changes in the *Lûle'vitûm*."

Asira chuckled, "Except for you, of course."

"Except for me," Lök nodded, and helped her with another sip. Asira was alive, safe, but Lök knew he would never be the same again. That wood – the home of the Eleaos'i – was a curse, or so it seemed. He feared just how far it would fall into the decay of time if it never changed.

An Orsain's Legacy

Eoras, Squire of Orphaeon

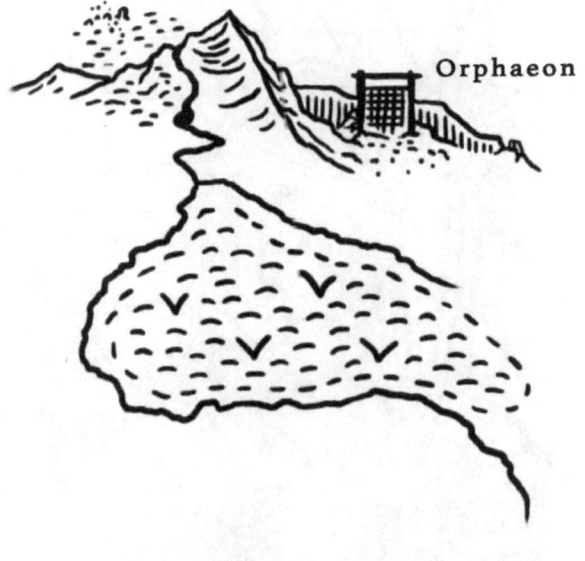

Orphaeon

*...being a short story during the Age of Origin,
approximately in the year 926...*

Eoras stood bored on the outer wall of Orphaeon. It was one of those miserable days, where the rainclouds over the Eurymyr occasionally shed the tears of Aegis over the fields, drowning them in haze and frost, as if She too had nothing better to do than weep through the doldrums. As soon as a bit of sun crept through the passing storms, by the time he'd dried, another cold shower burst from Her skies to numb them all again. She was a child in perpetual tantrum, and didn't stop as the sun set – all simply worsened. Freezing, watching the icicles form on the parapet, Eoras longed for the guard change at the height of the moons, and wondered if his so-called line of legend ever needed deal with such discomfort. Right now, his father, Hierarch of the Anvil City, sat leisurely on his cushioned half-throne in the Orphan Hall, most likely playing *isaro* with himself. He didn't sleep much of late, spending his days reliving the golden years of the Orsain, losing himself in the histories accounting their glory, instead of doing anything he himself would be remembered for.

Eoras, no matter that eminent lineage, was as subject to his frail father's command as anyone else. The process was pain-staking and would take half his life – Squiredom to Knighthood – just like his foresires. Of note, his great-great-great grandsire – *is that the right number of greats,* he thought, losing track, because he didn't much care – was Iödas, son of Eirdas. The mighty Iödas was the man who'd liberated the orphans of Thorncrest and bastards of Anvaer. He'd erected Orphaeon in its place, started and ended the Orsain Civil War, and began a legacy no one born thereafter could ever live up to, though all of them tried. Eoras was positive the history had been exaggerated, but that didn't keep it from being told over and over again by the people ... and his father. *What could Iödas really have done that was so difficult?*

It was the dead of night, fog heavy on the Fields of Eurymyr, when the nameless rider arrived. From the south, he rode, and reared a mare the color of ash and blood at the gates of Orphaeon. Before anyone could call down, the horseman called up, "Wrath is at my heels, and death arrives at your door – open your gates, I say, and make your defenses ready!"

Disarmed by the rider's boldness, Eoras knew not what to do, nor did any other guard. They looked at each other, bewildered, until the rider called up again:

"It is of perilous urgency I speak with the Hierarch! Oisin burns!"

Eoras realized the color of the mare was not its hair, but blood caked on from battle, and ash singed to its haunches. When Eoras lifted his eyes, trying to see beyond the fog to Oisin far away, what he saw made his decision. "Open the gates!"

The guards obeyed – even if he wasn't their superior, he was still royalty, and in cases of urgency, simpletons always followed the command of blood. The rider galloped in full haste under the portcullis and up the main road; his horse took the stairs to the Orphan Hall in one mighty leap and skidded to a halt. Its master dismounted before its hooves stopped clopping. Eoras was certain it was a Freemare, one of the noble line of Nûmyri raised in the holy stables of Oisin. Either this man was a Horselord or noble of the Thatched council in their sister-city, or he'd stolen it. However, the Freemares were not known to listen to anyone save their Freeriders.

He turned back to the sight in the distance, that had drove his hand and heart to open the gates.

"The fog, it moves toward us," a sentry next to him reported warily.

"I see it. It's not fog," Eoras knew. It was a long and wide cloud of dust that roiled, rolling forward on the horizon. There was no fooling anyone, now; he knew what happened when an army moved across a plain, it was in every story, but he never expected to see it for himself. There hadn't been political strife in the Realm since the Second Barrens War, a decade or so ago, when Eoras was just an infant. That was with the accursed Nithûr. Orphaeon and Oisin had been at peace for even longer. In fact, many called this the Eorlin Golden Age, but that was about to end with whatever emerged from the fog. The normal mists of the black eve shone bright under the height of the moons, but something else tainted them as the dust picked up closer and closer to the city. Horses hooves would've charged faster, so it was soldiers' feet, he knew – a lot of them. Beyond this mystery, tendrils of orange and red slithered and sparked like crackling firelight in a sea of smoke. It was as if a storm brewed from the earth, instead of the sky.

The height of the moons saw the guard change, but Eoras didn't move. He watched, and waited.

The nameless rider burst from the Orphan Hall, left the doors ajar behind him angrily. He remounted and galloped into the city's square, open for all to see afore the massive statue of Orphaeon's famed golden anvil. He reared the Freemare, who let out a deep and wakening whinny. The guards on the walls and in the streets watched from their posts, intrigued, while citizens gathered at their doors and windows, staring in awe. The rider stood in the saddle and hoisted himself atop the columned anvil. For the grandeur of his steed, Eoras saw the man was no more than a kid, now, in stableboy's clothes, torn with its fringes burnt all about. All in all, he looked as though he'd just stepped from a fire in a haystack. Then again, standing on the only monument of the city, he towered over them all: "Smiths and soldiers of Orphaeon!" he cried out, so all could hear against the silent night, "I come to you from Oisin, but tell you, your sister-city is no more!" A murmur ran through the crowds. "I rode out of my home sundered, and it will now be no more than ash if I'm ever to return." There was a sharp gasp and an indiscernible chatter of questions. The rider cut through them all. "Our enemy... We don't know why ... why our sacrifices have displeased him, have led him to our gates asking for our lives, but the

Wrathlord himself drives his rage toward you now."

"The Ninth?!" a guard beside Eoras cried.

"What did Cisin do?!" a woman from a nigh window shrieked.

"Again, we know not our transgression. Only the consequence. And I'm here to beg you – take up arms with me against him."

"Fight against one of the Eleven True? That's madness!"

"May be it so, but our only other option is to run with no hope of escape, cut down when caught up, or to cower and accept death as a punishment we know not the crime for. But, I say this to you!" He paused to be certain all were listening. "If anyone can stand against a god, it is the Horselords of the Anvil City!"

His charisma won him the crowd, the rallying cry met with thunderous applause. Contrariwise, Eoras thought it the stupidest idea he'd ever heard. Why would they stay to fight something that couldn't be killed?

The rider continued, "Send every child under the age of ten in train with their mothers north to Berth, and pray the Ninth will not take his wrath so far. The rest of you make ready!" Though the man had no real authority, the city bustled and made ready. Eoras wondered where his father was in all this – he couldn't have agreed to something so radical. He ran to the Hall to find out.

The Orphan Hall had emptied by the time Eoras arrived, its homeless either armed for battle and sent to the wall, or given provision and sent north. His father solely remained, slouched in his half-throne, staring at a pedestal nearby whose holy occupant was a blade of yore and ancient fame.

Eoras didn't wait to be addressed, "Father, how could you let some ragged stableboy rally our people for a hopeless cause? Where were you?!"

His father did not turn; instead, his gaze drifted, then fell to his son's feet, "Ah, my son, you should be on the wall."

Eoras knelt before his king, not out of respect or duty, but he had to look the man who once sat tall, his father now haggard and diminished, in the eyes, "Why did you not deny him?"

"Oh?" his father's eyes shifted noticeably, thinking back, "Oh, I did."

Eoras was aghast, "Then tell your people they're committing treason by following the cad!"

"Son, nothing would change. And I'd rather them die loyal, proud, honorable in a just cause, than traitors."

Eoras shook his head, "This is madness."

His father's eyes flared, and he finally caught his son's, blue on blue, and Eoras' heart froze. "This is war," the king declared, and stood. "And if only I were my grandsire, I would be out there with him, leading the charge." He walked to the pedestal, and his hand caressed the glass protecting the blade. "But, alas. Our line has fallen, my boy. And I am a coward. I encourage you to take back what glory you can, and make your foresires proud. Go now, and die with honor."

Eoras stood and pointed at the sword, "Those legends are exaggerated, and you know it."

"Do I? This blade was smelt from the same haematite that brought our people freedom."

"Iödas carried a spear into battle, not a sword, father."

"Aye, but it was Iödas' son who carried this sword in the First Barrens War. It defended Berth against the necromancers."

"It doesn't matter!" Death on their doorstep, Eoras couldn't believe he was arguing the lesser points of history. "We're all going to die today, because you won't order our people to flee."

His father sighed, and an odd glint of something Eoras had never seen before entered the old man's eye. It was as if he was remembering a vision of the past, a past he'd never played through for himself. "Have you seen that rider? There is something about him – kingly, it is, and they will follow him to any end. I have never had that spirit, that courage."

"That stupidity."

"You will follow him to any end as well, now."

"But, father—"

"As a son, obey your father. As a squire, obey your liege."

There was nothing he could do – as much as he wanted to run, he wouldn't betray his father, and he wasn't a deserter. "Yes, my lord." When he turned, he heard the glass shatter behind him.

"Son."

Eoras cocked his head back. His father had taken the sword from the pedestal. He tossed it to his son, who had no choice but to catch it, or allow the holy relic to clatter on the floor. "My lord?"

"Whatever your foresires are to us now – legends, myths, heroes. They did not fight to be remembered. They fought for freedom."

Every boy and girl, man and woman not on their way to Berth was either on the wall or in the yard, waiting. As it was named, the forges of the Anvil-City granted each soldier solid steel, and for that they were lucky. Luckier still were those mounted, but they were few and far between. The

Horselords were all dead, if this nameless rider was to be believed, and the stables to the south were no more, the Eurymyric cities burned in the Wrathlord's wake.

The rider kicked into the haunches of his freemare, and brought her up to stand atop the gate, standing a giant among men. The captains of the guard surrounded him now, all talk of tactics and defensive strategy. Eoras was stuck watching the cloud, queer as it was, creeping ever closer across the fields. When it stopped, the host was revealed in the moonslight.

The gasp on the wall echoed across the Eurymyr. Eoras had never seen a ghost before, but wondered if this was their ilk. The army bore armor fashioned on Orphaeon anvils, sent south to the Oisin Horselords, but it was cracked at the seams and across the plate. It didn't fall away as it should, but was held together by some eerie force, or possibly cauterized plate to skin... The skin... The night cleared, and the *evari* shone bright over the evil before them. It lit up the faces Eoras would never forget if he lived through this nightmare. "I may count myself lucky if I don't..." he whispered to himself.

"What?" the guard next to him asked.

"It's the Horselords. Or what's left of them."

Anthology II

"What ... what have they become?" the guard stammered.

Their skin was pale and grayed, as if decomposed, yet immune to rot. "Neither living, nor dead," Eoras postulated.

"But ... how?"

He didn't know, and he didn't want to.

"Their eyes..."

"I see them." They all did. Their eyes were the strangest of all, a clear-like, sunken socket that refracted the moonslight and glowed. These wraiths saw the world very different than the living, but not quite taken to Shadow. And they moved with a calm rest, as if sleep-walking in a dream romantic and terrible.

When the Wrathlord appeared, every soldier on the wall shifted. Their voices rose in panic, and a wave of dread washed over them. "Steady!" the nameless rider called out, but it did little against the tide. The god was something else entirely, and Eoras' mind could not find words to describe him mortally; as a living man, he could not seem to comprehend what he saw.

The captains of the guard did everything they could. They shot back to their battalions and started yelling. The orders passed through Eoras unheard, as he quite forgot where he was, what he was doing, and fell to his knees in terror.

The battle took a turn for the worse when the gates' hinges were blasted from their plates, and the large metal postern toppled into the yard. The lesser wraiths flooced the square, and the Ninth systematically prevented as many deaths as he could; instead, he would take them one by one, each on the verge of passing into Shadow, and chain them to whatever twilight state he'd brought the others. One by one, they were turned to his own violent purpose.

Eoras hadn't moved from the wall, frozen in fear behind the crenellation. He would rather be dead than one of those things, caught between life and Shadow. He wondered if this was damnation in its purest form. His foresires, as they were told, would have stood and charged into the fray without hesitation, but the thought of becoming one of those creatures immobilized him. Whatever Iödan blood ran in his veins was cold, whatever enemy blood ran down the blade in his hand was dried, and he could not bring himself to follow their footsteps. This battle was hopeless. What happened now, would happen, and there was nothing he could do about it. He felt the tears fall from his eyes and drench his cheeks, unsure if it was fear or disappointment wrenching his heart to despair. He wiped them away angrily – he was a coward, and his family's legacy would end that way.

Oddly, as he dried his eyes, he noticed a pair of black boots in front of him. If it was the enemy, he'd already be dead, so he looked up – a young girl, no more than ten or eleven, stood in front of him. She wore a maille hauberk too large for her, but her boots and leggings were her own, a second-year squire's honorarium – all Orsain women were warriors until they chose motherhood. This one, a child in war, stared at him motionless.

When nothing happened, Eoras finally asked, "What?"

"What's wrong?" she asked. She'd seen him crying.

"What's wrong?!" he flared, his voice cutting through the din of battle not so far below them. "Look around you, little girl."

"It's evil. Isn't that what you and I have been trained to fight?"

"You may be blind to this obvious flaw in your plan, because you're so young, but what you're trying to fight is a god."

"It doesn't matter what he is. It matters what we are. Who I am. I don't know much about war or battle or blood; in fact, I'd never seen death before today, never witnessed evil, but did you not take the same oath as I?"

"You're trying to win something you cannot."

"I'm not trying to win. If I was, I'd be afraid of that. Of losing. I'm only trying to protect my people, and at that I am succeeding, because many have escaped today to freedom."

"I... Aren't you afraid?"

"This isn't the dark. Or the unknown. Or the future. It's here. In front of us. Killing our friends. Our family. Why be afraid of it?"

"And of dying? You're not afraid of dying? Or being..."

"Turned into one of those ... things." The little girl shrugged, "I don't know. A lot of people die for lots of reasons that are stupid or silly or pointless. If I die today ... or worse ... it's not for any of those reasons, but because I fought. I'm doing what I should. I think that's all that's supposed to matter, right?"

She made so much sense, and Eoras hated it. He swallowed, "...Yeah." He'd focused so much on what his legacy told him he should be, so much on what he thought he couldn't be, he never thought about what he was – an Orsain. He was a guard of the watch working toward knighthood. And today, right now, he was a soldier, just like her, who needed to protect his people.

He stood, swallowing it all – the carnage, the ruin, the despair – and pushed forward. He saw a flash of light strike across the city as dawn broke through a muster of fire and smoke blanketing the horizon. Then, there was a horn. A horn bellowed across the Fields of Eurymyr. It drew all attention, and even the Wrathlord himself paused. Everything fell still and silent. Only one thing could have turned the god's gaze back to the Eurymyr – another of his kind had arrived.

Eoras wasn't sure if two Eldûn had ever been seen in a single place before. They kept to the Realms who worshipped them, and even then, were little seen. The haze of morning lifted, and there before the Anvil City was the most magnificent sight Eoras ever beheld – shepherds and farmers and commonfolk that could be none other than an army marching out of the Wreatheland from across the mountains were amassed and riding to Orphaeon's aid. Leading them was a man it seemed, in armor cracked and faded, a tattered cloak billowing in the wind, and a shepherd's crook in his hand. It was as if taking a page straight from the holy texts. The Eighth, the Valorlord, the Ninth's twin brother, had arrived to save them all.

The Ninth turned furiously back to the gate, and was suddenly without, riding a wave of fire and fissure toward the Wreathelanders. Eoras heard a cry from the yard he should've expected – the nameless rider was still alive and fighting, "Push them back! Push them back to the Fields, and let them be surrounded!"

Eoras wasn't sure if it would make a difference. In the end, pitting one god against another, with man against wraith around them ... it was nothing short of insane. "It doesn't matter," he said aloud, as he heard the freemare's heavy hooves gallop over the gate's ruin unto the scars of the Eurymyr, driving the enemy back. "I am a soldier. And I will protect what I stand for, until I can't."

Mornings to Eoras were usually cold and biting, but here in the heat of battle, he had never known such drive, such anger, such adrenaline. The very air, ignited by the Wrathlord's presence, seemed to fuel it. Unlike the vantage on the wall, where everything felt like the big picture, here on the ground it was very real, and very personal. It was one skirmish to the next, like a game of *isaro*. It was survival. A single wraith took a half dozen Orsain to counter, and they worked in tandem with the Wreathelanders to make a stand. Eoras wasn't sure if the wraiths could die, but they were falling and not getting back up.

Eoras caught sight of the nameless rider leading them all, charging through the hordes. In a sea of fire, his freemare was cut down from under him, and he tumbled into the chaos. Eoras broke free of his own skirmish, and pushed through the foray to reach the man. Miraculously, neither he nor the mare were dead. The steed rose from where she fell and reared, her breast bloody, but using her hooves as weapons in a bludgeoning barrage to protect her rider. When she whinnied, her cry echoed across the Fields.

The stampede followed. Not long after her call faded, a pounding resonated across the field, closing fast. On the horizon, dozens of horses charged from the East, herds from the Highlands, and crashed into the bedlam. They avoided each shepherd and soldier, trampling the damned.

Unfortunately, nothing would stop or stand in the way of the Wrathlord. The earth cracked below his footstep, and a web of destruction carved through the Eurymyr in a strike that swallowed everything it its path. Horses, Orsain, Wreathelanders, and Wraith were seen falling into the chasms. When the ground splintered beneath Eoras, he leapt away, and fell hard to the ashen earth. He caught a glimpse of the bottomless pit, of Aegis' womb, and his heart raced like never before.

Fight on.

Where the voice came, he didn't know, but it pulsed in his mind like a beacon to bolster his courage. He fumbled back and stood, right into the spear of his enemy. The wraith's corrupted metal scored into Eoras' rib, but his maille kept it from driving too deep. He felt the blood seep through his tunic and undercoat, but he didn't fall, and he wouldn't die. Not yet.

With the blade of yore, he sheared through the spear's shaft, and spun on his heels. The next blow landed heavy against where the wraith's kidneys would have laid if he were still a man. The creature cried out and stumbled back, where two Orsain and one Wreathelander surrounded him to finish the job. One, Eoras saw, was the little girl. She was also still alive ... for now.

Eoras didn't join them, for he caught sight of the stableboy again. He was sprinting past every chance to help another, and every opportunity to fight. Gritting his teeth, Eoras kept one hand on his side and followed. Their leader's destination was a stone amidst the chaos, where the Eighth and Ninth were locked in combat, god against god, Wrath against Valor. Eoras knew whoever prevailed would sign the fate of them all.

Unfortunately, the Valorlord was losing. Eoras saw a flash of light, a slash of wind, a spark of lightning that blew apart the stone. He couldn't see where any of it originated, from whose hand drove these powers of Aegis, but he did see the blast of fire and brimstone that brought the Eighth to his knees. The Ninth stepped over him, blind with rage, and rose his arm to deal whatever blow might end it all. Eoras was unsure if a god could kill another god, but he watched in morbid awe to find out.

However, before Wrath's hammer fell, the stableboy appeared behind him, and a glaive he'd acquired somewhere on the battlefield tore through the Ninth's chest, leaving a hole where a mortal's heart would reside. Eoras had no delusion, neither did their leader – no mortal blade could kill one of the Eldûn. However, the thrust's intent proved fatal anyway. Crazed, the Ninth whirled about and sheared off the nameless rider's arm at the shoulder. He blew the man away, and spun back to his brother, who took the distraction as was given. The Valorlord was on his feet again, and his hand sunk through the cavity the glaive bore. He grabbed hold of whatever lay inside.

Eoras couldn't pretend to understand what was happening, but he knew one thing – from losing an arm, their nameless king would bleed out if he didn't do something quick. He raced past the gods, suspended in their own world of immortal deliberation. He fell to his knees at the boy's side. Their leader was staring up at the sky, his eyes emptying of all light. Oddly, he was also singing:

"She, picking flowers by the moons,
Eurymyr, of shining grace,
Brushing strands of silver loom,
Through ghostly locks accomp'nying.
Behold this light, reflect thy lace,
Dance she did through wilting tomb;
I saw that light upon her face,
Heard evermore, her song longing.
So, Eurymyr, my Eurymyr,
My love, my life, my fear;
Is it you I fought for,
Or died for, my dear?"

"You're not going to die," Eoras said. Ignoring the possibility that an enemy could take him at any moment, Eoras threw off his armor and removed his surcoat. He knew beneath it all, he was still bleeding out himself, but he didn't care. "Well, you don't want the bloody part." Eoras tore away the stained, and used what was left of the coat to press and wrap the boy's shoulder as he could. Aggravation rose, as the precious seconds passed, "The bleeding isn't stopping, we need to cauterize it." Eoras turned back to the gods, and saw what he needed. "Oh, gods, I hate this." He couldn't believe what he was about to do. He grabbed the boy's face, making sure he was still conscious, "I'm about to replace this with something that's going to hurt a lot." When the boy didn't respond, Eoras slapped him across the face, "Don't die on me!"

The nameless rider nodded, and his eyes flicked to attention – he was still alive.

"At least it'll wake you up." Eoras left him, and maneuvered on his belly carefully, but swiftly, toward the gods – the object of his earnest was the Wrathlord's very robes. His cloak carried with it fire, a perpetual burn in its wake. When he neared the confrontation, he heard them, the immortal. It was a conversation he knew he shouldn't be listening to:

"Brother, they will never be us. Their hearts are their own, for good or ill, and we cannot want to change them. Remember our creed."

"Words."

"Binding."

"They are not worthy."

"No, they are not. That's what makes them mortal. But, they are Aegis', as are we. You have not forgotten this, Dûnkrath. Come back to us. Come back to me..."

Eoras tore a piece of Wrath's robes from its cindering end. It immediately began searing through his gloves. Whatever they were talking about, it kept their attention. Eoras rose to hands and knees and crawled back to their leader in all haste, and undid everything he'd done before.

He rewrapped the bandaging with the scraps of fire and pressed. No matter his bravery, the boy screamed. The wound cauterized quickly, but Eoras kept the robes pressed to the shoulder with his own hands until he knew it was done. He could smell the burnt flesh through his gloves. When he knew it was done, he forced the boy on his side, "Time to put the fire out." The rider rolled with him, and they sat there a moment in agony together. When Eoras pulled the scraps away, they were still warm, but had lost all active embers.

By the time Eoras turned back to the battle, it was over. The gods were gone, and only the ruin remained, scars across the Eurymyr. He lifted the boy across his shoulders, and rose to his feet. "There's nothing to do now, but count our dead, and reorganize the living."

"And clean this wound," the boy replied, "I'd prefer to live."

Eoras chuckled, "We followed you. Does anyone even know your name?"

"It doesn't matter. I'll be gone again soon."

"Don't want to be our Nameless King?"

They laughed together, until both realized how much it pained their injuries to do so.

A Myrman's Marrow

Pa, Twenty-Third of Thirty Three

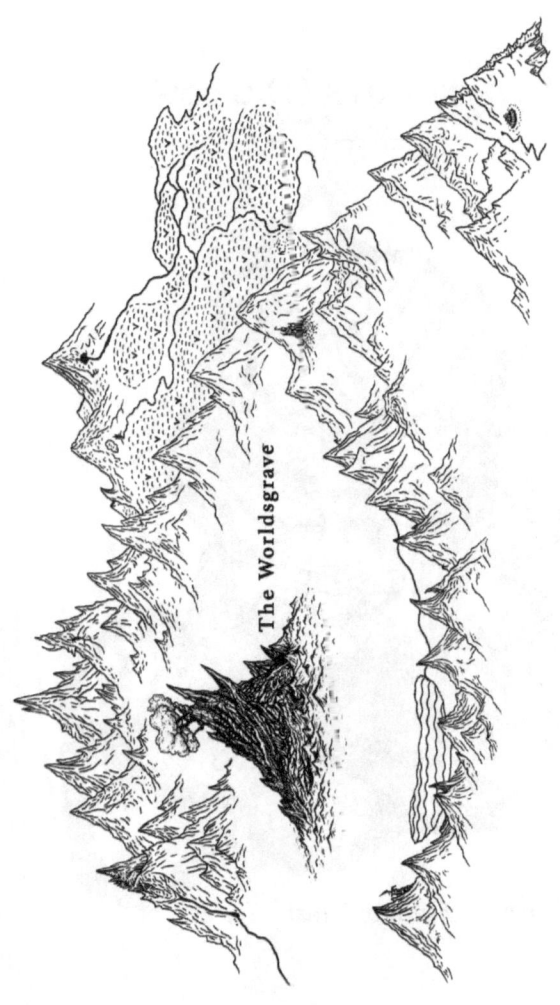

*...being a short story during the Age of Origin,
approximately in the year 926...*

Pa watched the gods retreat, leaving behind
a scarred wasteland where the Fields of Eurymyr
once grew wild and vibrant; it was now a mire of
blood-washed earth. At this distance, it saw the
cracks split Her flesh like a web of thorns, where
open fissures drove through the face of Aegis. Pa
wondered just how far they reached: *Is Her very
womb defiled?* it thought.

The Orphaeon soldiers collected their dead,
while the allied Wreatheland host made ready to
return home. Beneath the carnage, Pa caught sight
of a slithering in the sunlight – a tendril of black
mystery that writhed beneath the vestige of war
nigh a broken stone where Wrath and Valor made
their final stand, and the fate of both god and man
was decided. Pa knew something was amiss there,
and its curiosity got the better of it – it dropped from
the mighty fortification that was Myrhaven's
northern wall. "Where are you going?" Bain called
from behind it.

"Forth," Pa retorted in jest. Curiosity, in a
way, was its purpose, its name. Pa was the letter and

sound for "go for:h," twenty-third in the El'arria *myror*.

As the Myrmen were thrice the size of the other mortals Aegis bore, and born of the very stone of the mountain they called home, it didn't take long to descend the Spine of the World.

Pa crossed the Isdûn stretch, and passed the ruins of Oisin. It reached the Fields of Eurymyr without rest, and without wearying. *After all, a mountain does not tire,* it thought, *why should I?*

By the time it trudged through the ruin of battle, the dead were burned, and the Orsain were set upon rebuilding the gates of Orphaeon. The Horselords were too strong a people to let grief debilitate them; they would undoubtedly return stronger than ever to the Realms of Aegis, possibly decide to conquer, as that was the nature of mortals – to breed, spread, and 'civilize'.

Pa knew they could see the mighty Myrman from their walls, but they would assume it was here to take an account, a record of the battle for the Athenaeum's histories, but that would be put on Myr. It doubted any of them could tell the Myrmen apart.

Pa surveyed the Scars of Eurymyr until it spotted the stone ... and the slithering. It had grown, as if a body of some creature had festered from nothing before Pa's arrival. When it disappeared through a fissure in the earth, where a strange scar cut like a black bolt of lightning through Her flesh, Pa knew it had to pursue it. It reached the scene, the land melted and seeping into the subterranean, and saw the fissure there was just large enough for Pa to make chase. It fumbled through, large as it was, and disappeared off the face of Aegis into unknown depths.

Pa tumbled down a crooking collapse of rock and rubble, through Aegis' mineral and marrow, until it landed hard on a karst floor. It looked up, but the sun was lost far above. It heard the trickling of water somewhere in the black, but Pa knew it stood in a tunnel that could be none other than the Worldvein.

Nothing is meant to walk in this place, it thought, feeling a twinge of fear creeping up its spine of stone.

It saw two directions. Pa knew east led under the Stormstone Cascade, and the Evendain – the dark people who slaved for Aegis, those closest to Shadow... West led toward the Dûn'raeor, the Bloodrock, that which all believed held the heart or mind of Aegis Herself. No one really knew. It was a place no one dared to venture. It was passed down in the histories of the Fyrzhor that the Minds' Eye still imprisoned the living consciousness of the Aeonar, whose endless battle in the void created the world from the maws of light and Shadow. It was myth, but Pa knew there was truth in every fiction.

It followed the Vein west for leagues, hastening as best as it could through crook and crevice, climbing over or crawling beneath where the passage twisted and turned. At one juncture, it was forced to carve out a space large enough to continue, as Pa was nowhere near as small as the wretched thing it tracked: *Aegis, please forgive me; there is something strange here inside you.*

Eventually, the Vein opened, and a threshold was held up by columns of glittering schist, refracting an ominous, fiery glow beyond. Pa knew it had reached the Dûn'raeor, but hesitated. If it entered here, it was desecrating the most holy sanctum of Aegis. Pa spoke aloud to bolster its own confidence, "If She needs protection, I must go. Forgive me my transgression."

Pa stepped into the cavern.

At its center, spires of tantalum rose like a gnarled, corrupted crown of stalagmites. They were like fingers of a hand, crooking and skeletal, and the palm was nothing less than an abyss. Pa walked up and looked down, its eyes met a crimson horror beating in time and rhythm with its own heart. It was flesh, but not so, muscle and membrane, but not in form so much as understanding; it was fire lapping or caressing or abusing the same tantalum rising around it. The living fire was constantly melting and forging new links of a chain that appeared and disappeared in the waves of the spire's alloy. The chain held down the spirits of the Endless, imprisoned in this Minds' Eye – the fiction was fact, all of it.

Pa fell back, its mind racing.

Out of the Shadow, the creature it was tracking arrived. It crept awkwardly, quietly to the ledge of the pit, animal-like in nature. The earth rumbled in defiance, but could do nothing to stop it. The creature's throat let out a crack, as if it was trying to speak, but knew not how. Then, something changed. Something unnoticed or unheard by Pa made the thing cackle in perverse revelry.

Stop him!

Pa heard it through the tunnel, from the womb of Aegis, but it was too late – when the waves of alloy rose, like lungs taking in the sulfuric air in agonized breath, the creature reached into the abyss. He lifted the chain, searing into his palms, and without hesitation snapped the links in two.

Pa's senses blew apart. It heard the cries of anguish in a language it couldn't understand, a language even older than the El'arria: *But, there is no such thing!* Pa cried out in its mind, grabbing its pounding head.

Pa felt pain rending through its stone body, as if it was one with Aegis, and all the world was under attack. The Myrman fell to its knees, but kept its eyes on the creature. The horror took one end of the chain, shoved it through his bicep, wrapped it down his forearm, and used some power borne upon it by its sires to fuse it. A light flashed, and Pa saw nothing of how – but, felt a presence in the room released from imprisonment, then restrained again, bound to the chain, now one with the beast.

When its sight returned to it, Pa watched the thing snap the chain around itself like a whip. It tasted smoke in the stale air, the creature's flesh burnt and cauterized. Whatever happened was beyond the Myrman's comprehension; it was something unearthly and evil Pa had failed to stop.

The creature's form had taken on a grotesque, wrinkled man-like stature, bent in places it shouldn't, with tooth and claw sharp and bloody from its own accelerated growth. Its eyes glowed yellow, with a ring of fire and ash within. Pa could see the Wrathlord there, mutated and raging. It could see the Valorlord there, plotting and controlled. And it saw something else that terrified the Myrman. Born of both gods amidst battle, it was now a visage far from anything, but the carnage that spawned it. It was the manifestation of torment, the nature of chaos.

It is a broken child, Pa thought. *The Elven True are no more. A Twelfth Elzhri has been born.* It was terribly innocent, and the poor wretch had stumbled upon a power of absolute corruption. It now fed off the powers of Aegis and the Endless both.

And smiled.

It was a smile venomous and scheming. The creature limped forward, as if still unsure how to walk, but Pa was immobilized by fear. *I must do something; it must be destroyed before it destroys Her.*

As it neared, Pa found its strength. It rose, towering above the creature. It reached down for the thing's throat, and, oddly, it didn't move away. Pa's massive stone grasp wrapped around the grotesquerie's gullet, barely able to fit its hand between chin and shoulder. *Does its throat lengthen to fit my closing fist?* Pa questioned. The thing stared at the Myrman's hand with the same curiosity that brought Pa here.

The abomination's throat was strong, strong as any muscle of any god, so did not give in easily. It choked out a question through the collapse of its esophagus: "You ... *Myrain?*"

"Yes," Pa replied, thinking it strange the creature knew the name Aegis called it, instead of mortals.

"What. Am." The words escaped its cracked lips broken and slow, "This?"

It truly didn't know, and Pa thought he may be able to save it after all, "You are something else."

"It. I. We? What am it, now?"

It was confused with the spirit it shared with the chain. "You are the Twelfth," Pa answered, "Born of Wrath and Valor." Pa loosened its grip, but did not let go. *It may be possible to save this creature,* Pa thought, *hand it over to the Eleven to nurture for a better purpose.*

"I. Am. Blood," it spat.

"You are new."

"I. Am. Bone," bile ran down the edge of its mouth.

"Listen to me, you are—"

"Scars," it interrupted, and its arm snapped up, grabbing the Myrman's face.

How can its hand reach my face? It's too small. It's too far below me. The creature's form shifted again, twisted abnormally, as if fluid. Claw-like nails dug into Pa's stone-skin temple, and Pa cried out in pain.

"I. Am. Death."

Pa found itself on its knees: *When did my hand leave its throat?*

"I. Am. Life."

And how does it stand above me, now? Disbelief washed over it, and Pa looked up to meet the daemon's eyes glowering down. Nothing was stronger than the Myrman's might, until this moment.

"I am Fire and Shadow and Madness." A revelation dawned on the creature. "I am Chaos."

We are lost, Pa thought. He felt the creature push into its mind. It surged through Pa's body, and the Myrman felt the creature read its memories.

"Go forth," Chaos cocked its head, mocking Pa and grinning widely. "Yes, I believe you will."

Pa felt its own will slipping away. A darkness veiled its eyes, and it felt the fall of despair through its heart. *What this thing can do with me,* Pa thought.

Pa's hand dropped to the tunnel's earth, and its fingers caressed the womb of Aegis there in bare hope. The last words it chose for itself, before Chaos controlled its purpose, were said aloud, pleading to She who it failed, "Aegis, save me. Save me, please."

She won't. She can't, it rang out through Pa's mind. Pa lost all control. *She will burn.*

Anthology II

A Nûmunyr's Night

General Tristlen, of the First Bough

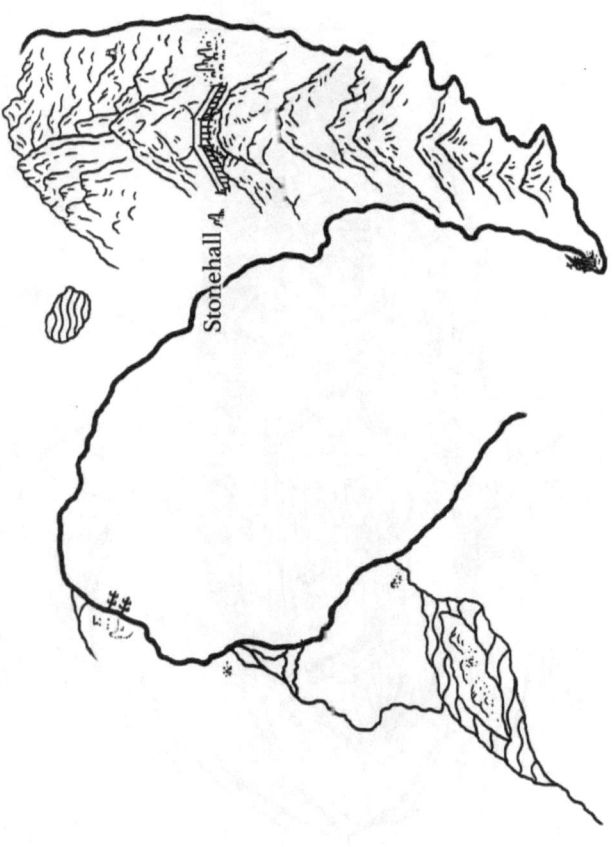

Stonehall

*...being a short story during the Age of Origin,
approximately in the year 964...*

During those brutal years of endless war –
nearly three decades of fire and blood – it seemed
every jack in the East shared a similar destination:
Nûmundor. The city of eleven trees, circled limb to
limb, arm in arm like brothers, stood untouched by
Chaos on the Eye of Wreathe, the isle amidst a fast
course and heavy rapids down the River Wreathyr.
In its center rose the Thrush Palace, hollowed out
and through with the blessings of Aegis, to bear the
boy, Thane, who founded this wonder of the Realm.
The twelfth tree always kept a torch lit in its rookery
in case any wandering soul – man or beast or bird –
needed refuge, and found their way across the
waters of sanctuary in the ever-night.

The jackdaw, called Tyntû by its masters,
landed in the rookery of the Thrush Palace, where
the Rookman knew all-too-well the message tied
about the little bird's talons. He saw Mistleton's
seal, and didn't bother removing it. Instead, solemn
and gentle, he addressed the messenger, "The city
has emptied, jack. There is no soldier left to send.
The King has taken his own gambit, now. If you

believe your words are of such importance, fly forth, and find him yourself."

He cradled the jackdaw in his palms, and led it back to the window. "East, I can say, to Cascade's End. But, I know not more. The King will be lost in snow and lightning by now." Tyntû chirped affirmatively, and the Rookman smiled. He let the jack fly.

Tyn soared back into ash-ridden winds, the Wreatheland below in flames. Nûmundor was only spared by the river, and the Rookman thanked the Eleven True for this blessing.

Tyntû took to the air currents northeast, through thick clouds of smoke, tainted black and red by war. He left the pyres behind him, where a wake of abominations led the charge of Chaos south. There wasn't a man or army across the Realms who'd seen a victory against the strange, god-like thing set upon a crusade of bedlam against Aegis. Hope was now rare, and faith nearly extinct.

The messenger crossed the stained Nyri, a bay whose waters were now carmine from the blood of a battle long lost; Tyn soared over traces of town and villages no more than spots of death and decay speckling the countryside; and he pushed on through every lonely cry in the night – survivors looking for others in despair. His stout and sturdy wings did not rest until he reached the rookery of Stonehall. The tower was small and gray against the overcast, overbearing backdrop of the mountains – it was nigh unnoticeable, now, in the snows beginning to fall. The jackdaw took to it graciously for warmth and refuge.

Unfortunately, the Rookman there gave the jack identical news; however, furthermore gave direction – a pass that led up and into the mountains. "You're braver than I, little one," he said, as he fed the jack a handful of kernels. "May you find our King well, and blessed." He released Tyntû moments later, as its jitters showed no sign of need, or desire to rest.

It wasn't long before a blizzard struck the pass, and threatened to freeze Tyntû's feathers; nevertheless, the jackdaw fought, and carried forth on wings of urgency. He would find the King.

Tyn dropped and drifted, was blown side to side by winds fierce and unforgiving; then, when he thought he could no longer keep from collapse, from dashing against the rocks, the jack's energy sparked anew – he saw the Thrushman camp. Leagues into the storm, on the western face of a mighty gorge, Tyn found dozens of tents burdened and bowing under a thick mantle of snow, with torches fighting as hard as his own wings to stay lit and flickering against the winds. As he neared, he heard muffled cries in the night – orders – and knew much was at work here. At the center of the camp was his destination. He shot into a cage left open for his ilk.

Tyntû hopped through a secondary layer of mesh to comfort on the other side. He stood in a large wireframe set on the tent's interior, just above a small brazier. He was immediately met by dozens of other jacks, and a few rather large, ominous-looking ravens he did not trust, in a twittering welcome.

The King's Rook was not like the others; he greeted Tyn with quick and rough hands, untied the message about his talons, then tossed him feed without so much as a look to where it landed. Tyntû's fellow flock allowed him first peck, knowing first-claw his weary state, before taking turns themselves. "Eat, drink, and warm yourself, jack," the Rookman finally sighed, as if disappointed, "It will not be long until we need you again."

General Tristlen waited patiently inside the King's tent, hands clasped behind his back, but forefinger tapping against his maille jerkin unwittingly. *Look at him, he thought, bent over that accursed stone again – it's taking its toll.* The Thrush-

King stared into the *raeordûmn* unblinking, hand clutching the object of power like a *göbel* to gold. The orb was discovered over a hundred years before, during Galaborne's Crusade, and many like the General who kept close to the King since its deliverance found themselves unnaturally long-lived. Tristlen was one of three on that crusade, knights too bold for their own good, and now one of few who knew its secret. Sadly, he knew very little beyond it, trusting the Heartstone even less now than he did back then. What it revealed in Galaborne that day – *the whitest knight of them all left to rot*, he thought – still sent shivers up his spine. However, he trusted his King. Every Nûmunyr did, wholeheartedly. Every Thrushman did, unwaveringly. Thane, King of Nûmundor, the Elder Lord of Thrush and Bough was the best of them. Thus, here Tristlen waited, amidst a blizzard, behind enemy lines, to believe in something more than himself.

Long moments in silence passed. Tristlen felt the heat of the embers at his front, and the cold of winter at his back. He saw the tent dip lower and lower with the collection of snow on its roof, and occasionally saw the odd snowflake breach the tent's flap. Each one melted immediately upon hitting the rug, but reminded Tristlen how soft the world could be. *Peace is no more than a memory, now,* he reminisced.

The Thrush-King removed his hand from the Heartstone, shaking. Tristlen didn't need to ask; Thane knew his question and spoke first, "Fire amidst snow. That is what I see. Death, a blur. A frozen wall and bleeding sun" He pointed to the message in his General's grip, "Seerhold?"

Tristlen shook his head sadly.

"The count, then, first, if you'll indulge me. To help bring me back to the here and now."

Whatever the King had lost to old age, he was as sharp in mind as a boy, but Tristlen found with each passing cycle that it was harder and harder for the King to discern between past, present, and future. Before addressing the most recent tidings, Tristlen did as bade – the count: "Marstead. Miresmarch. Reedstone. Rookstown. Featherfen. Gone, that we know of. The Ashlin have fallen, most likely purged. There is nothing left breathing along the Vesper Shores as far as the jack can fly. And the roads between Heather and March are sacked; reports say they've started to burn."

"And now?"

Tristlen handed over the letter, "Mistleton."

Thane took it and spit, "So, they *are* alive." He unfolded it, scanned it, and sighed.

Tristlen thought he saw the King attempt to stand, but failed: *Does his weakness finally show? Or is he just tired?*

The King tossed the letter to a pile of others, and considered the brazier warming the tent. "Faith. Hope. Instead of finding it for themselves, they give up, and desire it to be brought to them by others on the wind."

"But the town survives, sir. After all this time. If they can't break the siege of the conflux soon, they'll—"

"Starve," the King interrupted, and found his strength through anger to rise. "Yes, I know." He stared at Tristlen, who'd never seen Thane so quick to irascibility. "When fire fell from the sky, and Chaos struck the fields of the Wreatheland, where was Mistleton? What did the Croparchs do? Did they fight? No! They broke their *own* bridges, and hid. So, now, they..." he trailed off.

Tristlen worried; the King was on the edge of a very precarious ledge of sanity. He watched the old man recede, sitting back down and slouching. He teased his fingers through the tangled mess of gray and white bushel running rampant over his face. *I probably look no different,* Tristlen mused. Neither'd had a mirror in cycles. It had been a long walk, and a longer press on their hearts than their feet to get where they were. Now, they just waited for the right news – when to strike, when to do the impossible. "Templeton may yet stand," he finally offered.

The King grumbled, "Unfortunately, there is no telling what survives across the Spine, so our two hopes are still here and now. Luckily, Mistleton was never one of them."

"Seerhold," Tristlen acknowledged, wondering what had become of the great smiths of the southern mountains.

"And us," Thane said, driving his finger into a nearby table where a *scarborr*-skin map of the Realm lay. They'd inked in their current position, and battle plans were sketched all about it. He stared down, and chuckled in sadness, "We are left to think – what is there left to burn? Well, they can't burn the snow, and they'll never tear down a mountain."

This wove Tristlen back to the point at hand, "Has the stone given you the future, sir?"

Thane looked up, "I have long seen things before this stone came into my possession, General. You know this. I saw the birth of the Nûmundor I built. I saw the Crusade. And I finally saw where so many fatestreams misled my assumptions." He smiled, "They still confound me. This stone is merely another set of eyes for guidance. All I know for certain, is that we are here for a reason."

Tristlen nodded, "To make a stand, sir."

"To make a push!" He leaned over the *scarborr*-skin, the same *scarborr* that rent through Lamorek's leg on the first Crusade, before Galaborne took its eyes and it fled. Lamorek was the third of three, but, injured, was forced to return to Nûmundor; however, on the way back, he'd met his adversary again and finished the job. Thane pointed to a small dot on the easternmost edge of the Stormstone Cascade, looking out over the sea: "We take Stormhold, we cut the wick out from the fires of Chaos. Whatever communications drive those creatures down the realms will cease. This, I know, and have not misread."

"And maybe the tide will turn. If Seerhold could last until then..."

As if on cue, Tristlen saw Thane's eyes pass over his shoulder to the tent's entrance, where the Rookman burst in, "I'm sorry sir, but, Seerhold," he panted, out of breath, "They reply!"

Tristlen's heart was a torrent of emotion; he knew this would either give them hope, or sign their doom. He took the letter, and the Rookman took his leave. Tristlen felt his hand tremble much like the King's, but for dread.

It didn't take long to read. His heart sank faster than a ball of lead to river's bed.

"What does it say?" Thane asked.

For a moment, Tristlen's tongue was caught, his voice couldn't bear to deliver. "To ... to all still fighting – the Bellows are flooded. Seerhold has fallen."

"Good."

Tristlen couldn't believe his ears, but saw the smile spreading under Thane's beard.

The King knew he owed his General an explanation: "It's a sign, my friend. The one I've been waiting for. We are Her last hope. That means we have no choice – we push, now. And we win."

Three days later, the bridge was complete. The King's thrushes had flown across the chasm to tie the ropes, while the Thrushmen worked the wood and laid the planks. It spanned the gap between their current position and the range's farthest peak – that which held Stormhold on its seaside. They knew the layout of the fortress; it was a simple four-wall construct, thick, frozen, and surrounded by crags. A single gate faced the trade route to the sea, and that was the only way in or out. There was no other road around the mountain's backside. They would go unnoticed, descending from above and behind.

The Thrush-King stood next to the General, staring across the expanse, "We have all the fury of the Realms at our backs. This bridge is a marvel of war for the desire of peace, and marks the beginning of the end to this age. General, speak to your men, now, and give them what they need."

Tristlen turned to face the forty-two Thrushmen who'd survived the trek east, who'd endured the biting cold and the growing misery. He looked each in the eye through the blinding snow; it was amazing what a few words could do, so he chose them carefully. "Tonight ... you will do what the gods themselves will not. Tonight ... you will put your faith in the man standing beside you, and you will put your hope in your own heart. Tonight ... we are not the last line of defense, but the first line of offense! We are not here to win a war, nay, we are here to win a single battle – so that more may follow! Tomorrow... Tomorrow, the day will break, and so will they!"

The men cheered, though much was muffled in a sudden roar of wind that nearly knocked Tristlen off his feet. Thane patted him on the back and chuckled, "Your speech has moved Her, and the mountain replies. Let it be on our side tonight."

Tristlen sighed, knowing his next words futile, "I would not be your General without advising you to stay here, my liege."

"Ah, yes, well ... it's very cold up here, old friend. I am looking forward to the warmth of Stormhold's hearth. But, if I die," Thane pulled Tristlen close, a dire need in his eyes, "It falls to you."

Tristlen knew he spoke of the *raeordûmn*.

"It is the Heart of our people, and must be returned to Nûmundor safely. Do you understand?"

"Yes, sir."

"Tristlen... Don't listen to it. Ever."

Tristlen studied his King – there was fear, not for the battle to come, but for the years to follow. *What have you seen, milord?* There was something more the King desired to tell him, but wouldn't say it aloud. "I won't, sir," Tristlen affirmed. *To lock the thing away in the tomb-vault forever – nothing would make me happier, or feel safer, now.*

The Thrushmen crossed the bridge. On the other side, they moved around the peak, trampling through snow no man had ever set foot upon; they split into two parties of twenty-one. The mountain disguised their descent, its snow billowing up and around them as they half-stepped, half-slid down Her back. They were no more than a collapsing snow drift displaced in the night. Their momentum ceased when they tumbled to the base of Stormhold's plateau. They were positioned directly behind the fortress.

Immediately, Tristlen noticed Chaos was far cockier than anticipated – no fires were lit on this western wall; watching the mountain held no priority.

The Thrush-King's battalion broke off, and moved silently south around the perimeter crags. Of the twenty-one, half bore axes, half bore longswords, and all of them held a secret. Strapped to the backs of eleven, were a secondary defense – *kithes.* These massive tapering shields were forged in the fires of the Ilaeon, deep in the Bellows of Seerhold. Thane had bartered for them decades before, when he foresaw war in the *raeordûmn.* The Fyrzhor were not keen on parting with them, but Thane had his ways, an old friend named Syrvaritûmdor. Each shield reached six feet in height, spear-points at the shield's foot, and curved like a pauldron at its head. The other eleven men carried halberds, whose modified, elongated heads were separated from their shafts for travel. The shields would be drawn, and the polearms snapped together, when the time was right.

Whilst Thane faded into the fog, Tristlen's battalion stayed put, until one of his own returned:

"Walked the whole wall," Lönoral reported, "You're right. They're cocky bastards."

Tristlen patted Lönorel on the shoulder, and smiled, "So are we." The Lieutenant was the third son of Lamorek, and Tristlen had promised his old friend that the boy would stay by his side. Lamorek had already lost two sons to war. Tristlen motioned to the Rookman, who brought forth a handful of cages. When opened, dozens of thrushes, two and four at a time, nabbed knotted ropes in their beaks and shot skyward. They dropped the loops around the iced crenellation far above, then disappeared. They would circle the fortress in safety, now, until the gambit was successful. Or they were all dead. In that case, Tristlen had no doubt the thrushes would carry their King's body all the way back to Nûmundor for a proper burial, while the rest of them would be buried in the snow.

Tristlen led his men in scaling the wall, and was first over it. He knew Thane would watch, and wait for his signal from the Shadow of the mountain. He confirmed that nothing walked this end of the height; however, he saw a feral dozen beasts of man-like stature lining the perimeter on the wall looking over the sea.

One by one, Tristlen's men slit their throats, but nothing was heard in the yard below, for the blizzard's din howling down the mountainside covered their tracks.

The men reunited in a crouch above the gate, and peered down. Tristlen knew their blood boiled in the cold, hands drenched in abomination entrails; they were thirsty for more. Unfortunately, it had taken longer than expected – through the black of night and white of snow, Tristlen saw gray. Dawn approached, and with it the sun would reveal them all. He motioned to his men quickly, who moved to the braziers, and arrow racks filled with the tower's bite lining the parapet. *She is on our side. Our quivers will not empty,* he thought. They dipped their arrows in oil and flame.

He nodded to the Rookman – one cage remained at his side. He let fly the thrush within, and it floated down with elegance and grace to their King among the crags.

The little bird landed on Thane's shoulder, and he listened to its excited trills. "Thank you, little one. Now, find shelter, and keep safe from the battle to come."

The thrush obeyed, and Thane stood. The rest of his company followed suit, and as one walked forward. The storm knew their motive, and lessened, until the company was clearly visible from the gate's flanking towers. The heavy, laden postern creaked open slowly, until Thane saw the host of Chaos on its threshold. There were many reports of the tactics these creatures employed, and they were all counting on those reports to be well-founded. If not, this gambit would end very badly, very quickly.

At first, the host did nothing, eyeing the tiny company of Thrushmen who dared their gate. One abomination, smaller than the rest, stepped forward; it cried out in no language Thane understood. *And I know them all,* he thought. He assumed it was more emotion than speech, and recognized it as a threat or challenge.

He eyed the wall again, and saw the little flames at the end of their arrows draw back in string and yew. They were ready, as soon as the opportunity was presented. Therefore, the Thrush-King drew in a cold, steady breath, and clenched his shaking hand. Gruff and brazen, he called out in a voice that echoed through the pass, and carried to the host. "You will not see us run. You will not see us hide. We are Nûmunyr who stand before you now, and we are your end! We will purge your fire with fire, and see you buried in the snow!"

The creature that appeared their leader laughed a hacking fit, followed by his fellows in bellows of bedlam that literally shook the mountain. The earth beneath them rumbled in response, as if Aegis took a turn at the bout.

We are forty-two, Thane thought, *and they are hundreds, maybe thousands. We. Will. Win.*

The abominations charged.

As soon as the host was out of the gate, Tristlen held up his hand and whispered harshly, *"Hold!"* There was no room for mistake, no room for doubt. He waited until the host was within arm's reach of his King, and almost all were out of the gate. "Fire!"

The volleys were let loose.

The flaming arrows joined the breaking dawn in a raining fire that rid sky and snow of devil.

The moment the abominations about-faced to the arrows scoring their backsides, Thane called out to his own men, "Charge!"

His men crashed into the exposed enemy, and the fray was chaos, indeed. The Thrush-King was slower than his soldiers, but cut down each creature in his path with precision and efficiency. It didn't take long for the host to regroup and flank them, large as it was. "Back to back!" Thane ordered, knowing this was the end.

Eleven of the men drew back, circling their King. They dropped their axes and whipped out the *kithes*. The other eleven sheathed their longswords, and snapped together their halberds. Thane had trained them personally in this formation, for this single purpose, a single tactic – and when Thane saw them in position, he called out, "Down!"

The shield-guards speared each piece of defense into the rocky earth, dug in with all their strength, and buckled down. Simultaneously, the inner circle knelt behind them, halberd angled skyward. From on high, it would almost look like a pin cushion. The abominations smashed into the circle, attempting to use their numbers, their weight, to overwhelm the bearers, to break the circle, but the Thrushmen stood fast – eleven brothers to hold the line, with eleven behind, to pierce and impale. And at the center of it all was their King, standing fearlessly as the twelfth tree always had in Nûmundor.

The creatures' apparent captain vaulted over the dying, to the hole at the very top of the shield-dome – his target: Thane. The King saw him coming, but had no time to respond – midflight, an arrow blew through the abomination's chest, and it collapsed in a heap at Thane's feet. The King looked up at the wall, squinting in the sunlight; Tristlen's archers were relentless, and would not let up unless they ran out of arrows. While Thane's elder eyes could not discern his savior, he knew only one man could have made that shot.

Tristlen had no idea whether he'd made the shot. He prayed to the Eighth the mark rang true, but the dawn was blinding them all. Luckily, the creatures wore no steel, so if it was black, moved, and didn't glint in the sun, it was something to kill.

"General!"

Tristlen whirled around – a battalion had broken back from the host, and was now rushing up the stairwells of the nearest towers to confront them on the wall. "Split!" he ordered.

Two men went with him, while another two broke away with Lönoral. His men, and those with Lönoral drew blades, while he and his Lieutenant stopped a few feet back from their guards to notch another pair of arrows. The marksmen fired between their soldiers, as those at the head attempted to block the abominations' from passing the stairwell's summit. Keeping them bottle-necked was the only way to keep them from overwhelming the archers at the gate. To any layman, it would have seemed like madness to fight in such close quarters while arrows flew past your shoulder, but the men trusted the marks of Thrushmen bows.

One of the soldiers with Lönoral fell to a wolf-like mutation, which quickly bounded past the dead and ripped into Lamorek's son. Tristlen couldn't take his aim from his own well, so he cried back to the gate, "Left flank!"

The left side of the wall turned all bows on the stairwell and fired.

Tristlen cleared his stair, and turned to the other. He sprinted around the perimeter to where Lönoral lay, but the boy was gone. He cursed himself ... he'd promised – he shook his head: *It is not in vain.* He ran back to the gate, where his men had stopped firing.

Below was death piled high and black over the shield-dome of *kithes* standing tall. Even in the blood of Thrushmen, and bile of abomination, the steel shone through the bleak horror against the dawn. He counted the shields – eleven, as it should be.

Tristlen's men ran down to the rocks, and it was midday before the bodies were cleared, the men beneath able to move again. He held his breath as they stumbled to the sidelines, collapsing, exhausted, but free. The count: Two were injured, but alive; only one was dead. However, the deceased had plunged his defense so deep, that when he fell against it, his body held it upright. The General's heart rose, and let go of the breath he held, when he saw his King. At the legion's center, he stood alive and well, eyes closed, breathing slowly, with snow gently collecting on his beard.

Thane filled his lungs with the cool, refreshing air of freedom, but appreciated the sun that warmed his skin. When he finally opened his eyes, his men were taking their time to recover, and Tristlen knelt before him. "Milord, we ... we won."

The King saw tears in his General's eyes. He gripped Tristlen's shoulder, as a few thrushes came back down and rested on his own. He wiped away the man's tears. "Set the defense, General. We need to discover how this Chaos receives its orders, and prepare for a counterattack."

Tristlen nodded, stood, and ordered his men inside to occupy Stormhold.

Thane looked out to the sea. The thrushes on his person prattled, and he responded, "Yes, yes, I know. I will not take it for granted. The day is won. This host is the first to fall in the turn of the tide."

Anthology II

A Shard's Shame

Shyrkûr, Second to the Star

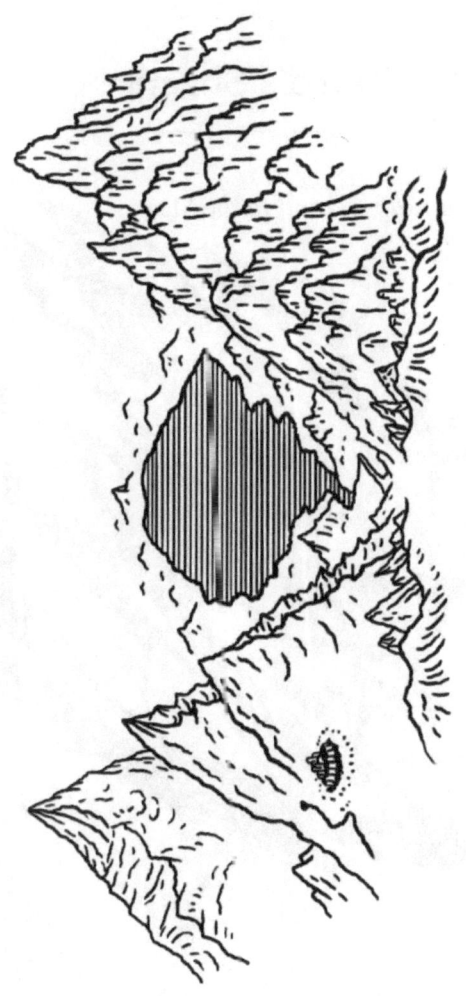

*...being a short story during the Age of Origin,
approximately in the year 965...*

It's not as if they could be defeated. After all, they were gods.

The Astar were the first of the Eldûn, the closest to Aegis; it was they who gave to Her the El'arria, the world's voice – a language and liturgy spoken, written, and sung for a thousand years. After the Beginning, the immortal race, manifested as conscious Glass, great and powerful, wandered directionless ... until now. Now, as fire rained down over Aegis' flesh, when Chaos born of Wrath and Valor drew its talons like sharpened brimstone through Her veins, deep into Her sacred womb, the Astar found a new purpose. It was finally time to prove their worth to Aegis again.

The Eldûn had never waged war before this day. They'd only witnessed it from afar. They despised what always fueled it – man's desire for such trivial things as wealth or power, reasons Shyrkûr never understood. *They are such simple creatures,* he thought, *and look how easily they bleed, how fast their life can be taken away. They are weak.*

Shyrkûr knew it was omnipotence that bred whatever ignorance kept them from understanding man, but now the Astar followed him without reserve, and fought alongside their Nameless King for a common cause.

The Nameless was a man like no other. While the rites of old had been lost to mortals for some time, he spoke to Aegis, and She whispered back her need of him in dream. When he came to the Eldûn door, the Astar found his cause just and true, and one that all creatures of the world rallied to, now – the Twelfth of the Eleven needed to be stopped.

The feeling it sparked through the Astar thereafter was like no other. Shyrkûr took a sick pleasure in shredding through the abominations of Chaos like a man's sickle though wheat-stalk. It was so easy, so gratifying, but he wondered: *Why won't their master show his face?*

The ice cracked beneath Shyrkûr's feet, but there was nothing to fear – the Isdûn, once the largest lake of the realms, was now frozen solid, and it would not give way. Tyr'draeor of the earth-changers made it so. He of the Ildraeor, second of the Eldûn races, flew with them, above them. He'd also refused to stand idly by and watch Aegis burn. On this gray and grimly day, he'd given them a battlefield that would not fail them.

It had cracked only because of the Astar's size – the height of the tallest tower of man, and fashioned of Aegis' crystal. They had a strength and stature of a true god, unlike the accursed Elzhri, who took the visage of man and refused to fight. Nevertheless, Shyrkûr knew they were watching, somewhere, repeating their ridiculous creed in the haven of their Shadows:

Interference with those beneath us is strictly forbidden...it is man's world, and we are to have no claim in its future.

And yet! It was the Ninth's betrayal of this creed – when the god came down in all his Wrath upon mortals, only to be stopped by his brother – that birthed the Twelfth in the first place! The Elzhri refused to take responsibility for their mistakes, always returning to their hypocritical diatribes. Shyrkûr shook his head, and swept through another battalion of horrors on the eastern flank: *Thus, the world has been left to those who suffer for it. But, we will make it right.* The Astar believed only in common sense. *Gods need no law,* Shyrkûr thought, *in the end, we are all children of Aegis.*

He saw Myrkûr, King (as any mortal understood it) of the Astar, inspiring the hearts and hopes of their allies from the center. He led the charge with the Nameless, who stood beneath Myrkûr, and raised his sword arm high. He cried out in their ancient tongue, "*Pa! Kain ö eli in hesdûn, pa! Röskyr ae evenrûn!*"

Another wave of abominations swarmed Shyrkûr, but the cry of the Nameless King drove him on. Shyrkûr reveled in each triumph, found himself lusting after each slaughter of nightmare threatening the livelihood of Aegis. He knew each movement he took was another reflection of the Astar's limitless power. *We could probably win this battle ourselves,* he thought, *but it is good we are not alone.*

Orsain cavalry broke through the lines and joined the offensive, helping Shyrkûr clear the eastern flank. He was impressed by the ferocity of man, the tactics and bravery of things that could so easily perish. It was rather hard not to step on them, in truth, but Shyrkûr didn't mind. *We will win the day, god and man together, for Aegis.*

In this all-too-certain victory, Shyrkûr was the first to see Chaos break through the clouds and join the battle. Somehow, some way, the unholy creature had tamed and enslaved one of the Ildraeor, Fyr'draeor – the guardian of the Evar'nûm – to be precise, and now saddled him, an evil champion on corrupted wings. *No wonder the Twelfth stayed hidden for so long,* Shyrkûr thought, *what is this thing?*

The answer, of course, was very simple. He was the manifestation of Chaos, of madness incarnate. Aegis, surely, was crying for retribution over this creature's transgression.

As the abominations could not rightly harm Shyrkûr, he watched the Twelfth – or Syrsevar, as the creature was so named – descend. Syrsevar drove his mount into Tyr'draeor, and the kin clashed, all teeth and talon. Exactly where he wanted to be, the Twelfth leapt from his slave's back, fell through the air with a plot no living thing could have imagined or countered; his target was the King of the Astar: Myrkûr.

In his descent, Syrsevar drew some unholy chain of holy tantalum from his fleshen sheath, a grotesque extension of his unearthly reach. It lashed out, and cut through Myrkûr's crystalline crown. It snapped back and struck again, when he landed atop the Astar.

The chain forged in the fires of Aegis' womb, in the very Minds' Eye that kept imprisoned the Endless, shattered the King of Glass into shards that scattered across the Isdûn in fragments of broken divinity.

Panic rose in the hearts of all: *Had this thing killed the first of them all?* It was impossible! *But how?!*

In this moment of terror, as Myrkûr's shards rained over the battlefield, Shyrkûr saw the creature for what he was – a god, truly, one whose only desire was to destroy for the sake of destruction. In that moment, Shyrkûr also came to the only conclusion he could – the battle was over, the war was lost, because one god would never be enough to satisfy Chaos.

Syrsevar snatched up the rib of Myrkûr's shards, and fused it to the chain about his arm. He slammed the rib's spear-end into the field of ice, but not just to pierce the lake.

In less than another moment of time for the immortals, cracks split and webbed across the frozen tract. The Twelfth's cackling followed the crackling ice, as it reached the feet of every Astar. Shyrkûr watched with a broken heart, knowing all too well what would come next. He couldn't bear to watch those he loved perish; therefore, he looked down between his own feet, to meet his own fate, the doom of them all, head on.

The fissure beneath him sent a crack up his leg, and Shyrkûr felt the splitting of his crystalline skin like dried flesh in the sun. Then, he felt his body splinter. *Is this death? Can I die? Aegis, hear me now! Save us!*

Aegis did not respond. The certainty was all he knew in the end, and wishing not to see this end to any further madness, Shyrkûr gave in.

And he shattered.

All Shyrkûr wanted to be was dead: *Whatever that means.* But, he wasn't.

They were gods, after all. *We were – are – immortal. We couldn't – can't – lose.* How wrong they were. *No, we just couldn't – can't – die.*

What is this feeling, now?

Am I here?

Or there?

He could hear more than he ought, thoughts of his kin, but they were scattered – *No, I'm...*

...scattered.

They were still connected; he felt them, but couldn't move to them.

I can't move!

Why can't I move?

This couldn't be.

What has been done to me?!

To us?!

He cried out, but through the air found silence. He only felt the cry of the other shards around him. They were one, as they had never been before,

Or have always been...

The voices ... so many.

I am not alone.

I am not alone.

I am not...

...alone.

He wasn't sure who else, if anyone, anything, or even Aegis heard him – them – anymore. They were lost, but, he could see the sky.

Why can I see the sky?

I am fallen.

Why can't I get up?

The voices ... so many, so loud, so wrong. It was rampant, and continued through the night and the coming day. He felt like he was weeping: *Am I weeping?*

I cannot weep.

What does it matter?

Nothing matters.

Years later, he still felt like he was weeping. Centuries later, he heard himself laughing. In the new Age, he'd find himself mad.

The Astar did not learn for another thousand years what ended the Battle of the Isdûn. They never knew the Elzhri who took a stand in their name, or the Nameless King who cast down Syrsevar from the Tower of the Evenrûn. That, when all was said and done, the council of Eleven True imprisoned Syrsevar forevermore, and did take responsibility...

No, the Astar would not learn these things before it was too late, before they found themselves lost to a fate crueler than death, and deeper than insanity – immortality as Shards.

A Fyrzhor's Fate

Iltvyrishyrdûr, Envoy of Seerhold

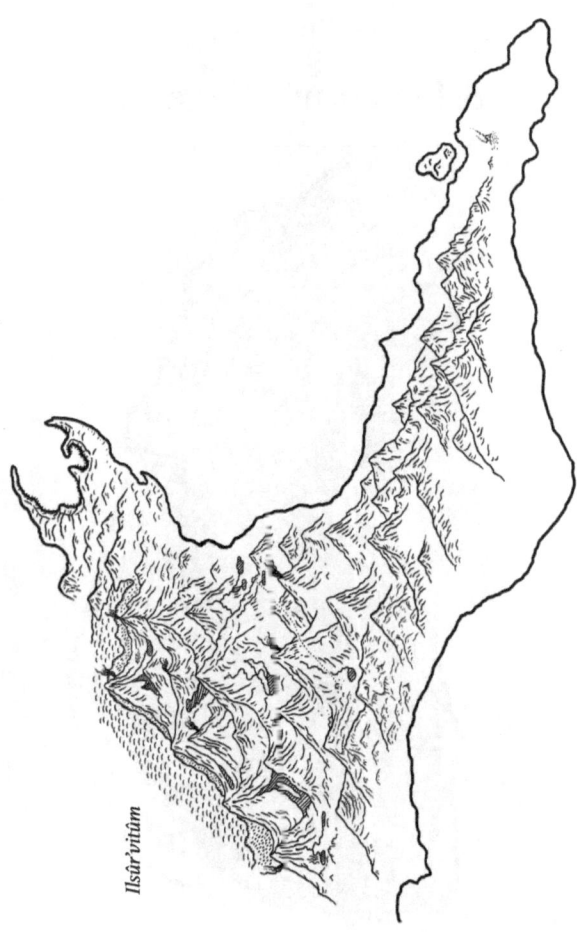

Ilsúr'vitûm

*...being a short story during the Age of Origin,
approximately between the years 966 – 967...*

Kirdûrikasdûmn watched the flame take his
brother's flesh unto Shadow, a funeral pyre no
greater seen by gods or man, noble or common. As
Fyrdûr, the Black-King, Kirkas was at the head of
the mass, but knew behind him, the Ilaeon Forge
was packed with soldiers and smiths, cooks and
clerics, growers and gardeners, all paying their
respects. The Holy Vicars sprinkled a powder
across the coal that set the fire's smoke to white. It
fed by flue up through the mountain, until released
at the volcanic peak, so all the Cinderstride would
see and know – a mighty hero has fallen this day.
However, Kirkas thought, *that's only if there's anyone
left out there alive to see it.*

The battle that took his brother's life was
only a single, albeit defining, moment of triumph in
an otherwise hopeless war. The abominations of
Chaos were defeated here, the peaks of the *Ildûm'tyr
Ritûm* purged, but elsewhere... As King, he needed
to know the fate of Aegis; but for now, as a brother-
in-arms, Kirkas led the funeral procession in
chorus, to return the ashes to Fyrnûr Bay whence

he was slain. Their voices echoed through the
Bellows, proudly deafening:

> "High above and far below,
> The mountain calls — we follow;
> The hammer strikes, the anvil sings,
> The blacksmith borne to steel-rung wings.
> O'er the wall of the High One's Hall,
> Never, nevermore to stand tall!"

> "Fallen, now, is Fate's design,
> To the evari align;
> May his gauntlet grip the sky,
> Helm and hammer, there will shine.
> 'Pon the wall of the High One's Hall,
> Never, nevermore to stand tall!"

> "Here on Aegis, walk no more,
> Ne'er to fight, and ne'er to forge;
> Here on Aegis — into lore,
> Etch'd into the Book of War.
> For the wall of the High One's Hall,
> Never, nevermore to stand tall!"

They reached the bay, where Kirkas'
brother's ashes were lain with his armor and the
spearhead that killed him, all within the small
shyrdaindûmn, an iron, nine-pointed, casket of sorts.

It was lowered into the earth at the exact place the Fyrzhor had fallen.

Kirkas' voice was not just one of dozens, now, but thousands en masse that joined them from their place of work or play through the passes of the mountains and around the bay's ring:

> *"His flesh has gone, his body burn'd,*
> *His maille to rust, his plate return'd;*
> *Beneath Shadow – above star,*
> *His name be known now, long and far;*
> *On the wall of the High One's Hall,*
> *Never, nevermore to stand tall!*
> *Never, nevermore to stand tall!*
> *Never, nevermore to stand tall!"*

The tomb was filled, and a plaque was laid over it wrought of steel, ornamented with strips of igneous rock glittering in the moonslight.

The ceremony complete, Kirkas turned to the Cinder Daughter standing beside him, "Walk with me, my love." Her name was Iltvyrishyrdûr, High Vicar and Emberfaith to the King. She'd been his better half for seven decades, now. "It is imperative," he explained to her, as they retreated to a path turning back to Seerhold, "You learn what's happened to our world. I trust no jack o'er your eyes." The Fyrzhor race were rarely seen outside their volcanic expanse, and when they left the *ritûm*, it was the Cinder Daughters who were sent. They were the eyes, ears, and hands to their male counterparts regarding trade, parley, and reconnaissance. It also helped that they were the size of a normal man, instead of the meter-and-a-quarter that was common for a Fyrzhor male. The only time the dredgers themselves left the Bellows were during times of war, or when the Fyrdûr was needed for an envoy of emergent peace. This would be neither: "If the world be lost," Kirkas continued, "There is much we need do to keep our sons safe, and homes hidden. Follow the fires north 'til you find something, anything alive."

"Shall I bring a contingent?" she asked.

"No," he shook his head, braids rattling through his beard, "A single Cinder may find her way easier than a bed of flames amidst bedlam fires. Avoid conflict at all cost, and come back to me alive, my love."

She knelt, so he could take her face in his hands. He kissed her forehead long, but lightly, a gesture that measured its affection in subtlety, rather than passion. Then, he watched her go. The King had just lost his brother, and could only pray to the Ninth he would not also lose his wife.

Iltvyrishyrdûr stood on a ravine's edge, the Withering Deep, the rim of the Black-King's Realm. Behind her, the *Ildûm'tyr Ritûm* rose hauntingly quiet, not a single eruption down the volcanic expanse in hours. *They are quiet,* Iltshyr thought nervously, *Aegis is lost.* The strangest were the clouds, hiding the moons, billowing black above the mountains, as if producing their own smoke. *Is She settling into this bed unsettled?*

In front of Iltshyr, to the northwest, the clouds were thinner, and the stars shone into the Withered Deep. This ravine led to the *Ilsûr'vitûm* (ironically translated to Ashwood) that, indeed, looked no more than ash, now. The dark forest was a fraction the size of what it once was, but she plunged down the ravine without a second thought on the matter.

She crossed the Withered Deep, and entered the darkling wood with hope in her heart that something must have survived.

That, she found. Many of the trees, though charred with branches broken and leaves burned away, continued to stand against death unyielding. The trunks, though a Shadow of themselves in survival, refused to succumb to the fires of Chaos that, just weeks before, engulfed the Ashwood. The blackened forest was made evermore eerie in the moonslight; for this, she saw the spiders long before she heard them. Their silent legs and bulbous bodies cast leering silhouettes on the forest floor from the cindered canopy of their reign. These horrid creatures that infested the wood lost much in the fire, and Iltshyr knew it would make them brash and bold – still, she did not fear them. They were petty creatures, and they could not touch her.

An overly zealous menace lowered slowly, barring her way, spinning its web between two trees on either side of the path in front of her. The silk was as thick as rope, and the arachnid was twice as fat as Iltshyr was tall. When it rotated gracefully on its strand to face her, the thing's eyes, all eight of them, met hers. She was already stopped. She neither wanted to destroy the beauty of its architecture, nor go around it. The brush burnt away, to use another path would be easy, but a mistake – there couldn't be a moment in which her eyes or body showed fear, or else they would see the Cinder Daughter as food, after all. As it was, a spider's eye could already see far longer, far deeper, than any other of Aegis' children. Each of the eight pupils, each of the irises, had a different purpose, and each of this one's studied her, while its eight legs twitched and measured what to do about this silent confrontation.

Iltshyr did not look away, did not blink, even when she noticed the Shadow of a lurker descending behind her. She was flanked, and if it had a man's breath, she'd no doubt have felt it on her neck. She gritted her teeth under pursed lips to keep her jaw shut tight. A single, raised brow was all she offered to convey that she was not amused.

One of the cocky one's eyes flicked over her shoulder – there was a transaction between the foe in front and the foe behind. Subtle vibrations disrupted the webbing. *Is this a language? Are they actually communicating through the web?* It astounded her when she thought about it, though it didn't take long to resolve; the one behind her disappeared, and the one in front bent low its head, avoiding the Cinder Daughter's gaze, now, as if apologizing. It used four of its legs to lift its recent masterpiece like a curtain.

Iltshyr didn't hesitate. She passed under the silk canopy without looking back, and not a single Shadow followed her thereafter. She wondered who the cocky arachnid was, but would never find out; however, her effect on him was greater than she could possibly imagine in the years of change to come.

Moons fell, suns rose, and rain washed enormous volumes of ash into the rivers of Aegis, choking the waters from their banks, causing partial floods across the already swamp-ridden Wreathemire. She passed villages and farms either abandoned, or razed to their supports; however, above all these unfortunate ends, swelled a strange beginning that disturbed her greatly – an unnatural fog lay over the land; it didn't lift with the fleeting day, or falling night. While it did not hinder her breathing, as smoke would, or smell or taste of anything, it did thicken in stretches so badly it forced her to maneuver around pockets of the dark and terrible enigma. She couldn't fathom a reason for the fumes without finding their source.

More unexpectedly, she found Mistleton, the famed village of stilts and struts, very much alive, and intact. When she reached the conflux that was the culmination of the North and South Wreathe Rivers, she walked the perimeter of the town, but found every bridge across the rapids collapsed. She knelt at one of their wooden posts, and considered it. Along the frame, she felt a latch unbroken, but missing pins at multiple facets pulled from elsewhere. *This was machinated,* she thought, *they did this – they hid.*

Iltshyr stood and called across the water's turbulent course to a timbre wall, "To the Lord of Mistleton, as I presume cordially your title here to be, I ask for council." She waited, and heard with the acutely-trained ears of a vicar of Seerhold something transpiring behind the wall. At length, a scruffy-haired Wreathelander, starved by the looks of him, poked his head up from the rampart: "Oh, my!" he cried when he spotted her, and vanished again. He'd immediately recognized what she was – a legend, as all Fyrzhor were, to most of the eastern world.

Iltshyr waited a long while, unmoving. Her training was one of control – over herself and others. Patience lent to that perfectly. That's why the Cinder Daughters were used by the Fyrzhor for such things as this, and why the Fyrzhor always got what they wanted.

Another man, lanky, but tall with the air of power, the eyes of ambition, and the stance of experience appeared next to his guard. "Are you indeed what they call ... what is it?" he turned to the guard, "Right – a Cinder Daughter?"

Curious. To not know what she was by sight alone, he must've been born across the Spine, a child without the stories of the Cinders: *What is he,* she thought, *a Reignman? How does he find himself leading their ilk?* "My name is Iltvyrishyrdûr, envoy of the Tower Black, Emberfaith to the Fyrdûr, and acting Speaker for the Cinderstride."

The scruffy man whispered into his master's ear.

"Fyrdûr – that is your King?" he asked.

She nodded, "I am his, and he is mine."

The man raised a brow, surprised at her candor, impressed by her equality. "Fascinating. I am Maleus, the title I bear is Croparch, now, not Lord, if titles please you. Quite frankly, they no longer impress me." He spread his arms, "I welcome you to the ghost of Mistleton, the capital of a long dead Wreatheland."

"How stark," she replied blandly, "Must I ask to enter here, to break bread with thee?"

"Ah, there we have a problem, I'm afraid. The bridges – the only way across the conflux into our dear, little town – are still being repaired. I am sorry for our current inhospitality, as our current is quite inhospitable." He was amused with his own pun.

She wondered if he'd lie to save face, it's what most men would do in his case, "What happened?"

"They came. We hid. They moved on, and for a while we thought ourselves safe. Only recently did they return: however, they did not stay – just blew past us, killing many and damaging more, but fled north it seems. Surely, you see it as a coward's tactic on our part, and I would agree," apparently, he was an honest man, "But, we are alive."

Iltshyr nodded, pleased with his decency, "I am not here to pass judgement, Croparch, only to seek knowledge. I would know what's happened to our world, and who survives. It is good to see that you do."

Maleus nodded, a genuine, pleasant smile cracking sunburnt lips, "In that case, Cinder Daughter, go to Myrhaven. We've had a jack from Nûmundor – the Thrush-King calls all leaders of men to gather under the Athenaeum's neutrality, so the realms can decide as one what to do about this growing Shadow mantling our world."

Odd, she thought, as Seerhold had received no jack. Granted, the Fyrdûr had outright lied to that Thrush-King already, claiming Seerhold had fallen (before it had actually fallen, then was taken back, a whole manipulative ordeal, really, that she would face later); therefore, the man probably thought all the Cinderstride was leveled. "To Myrhaven, then."

"If they can wait, please, tell them Mistleton will send its envoy as well. I cannot leave my people yet, not after that second coming, but I would like to attend. Once they feel safe and secure, I will be on my way."

"I will do so, friend, and I will make sure they wait."

"Thank you, Cinder Daughter.   With respect, I wish you luck, as you may very well need it. From the heights of these walls, we've seen many a strange thing stir beneath this otherworldly fog. May the gods be with you."

Iltshyr nodded, and was on her way, but not without a devastating reminder: *Where are the gods in all this?*

For Iltshyr to reach Mt. Myrkûr, it took far longer than any should recount the length of here, but, eventually – through parched valley and seared heather, scorched field and smoldered forest – she found herself climbing the holy stone steps to the Athenaeum.   Carved centuries before by the mighty Myrmen, they led up a straight, wide path to the gates of the greatest library known to Aegis.

One of the sentient stone sentries bellowed down from the wall, "Cinder Daughter, you are a long way from the place of your purpose."

"It is my purpose that brings me here. With respect to the *Myrain*," she used their name in the El'arria, "I ask for shelter, knowledge, and to have a seat at whatever this council is hereupon the ending of our age."

The doors, rising high as a hillock and as thick as a willow's trunk, opened wide, and another of the mythical gargantuans greeted her with open arms, "Forgive Bain. You are, of course, welcome here, Daughter of Aegis. I am Ama."

This time, she bowed with equal courtesy, "Iltvyrishyrdûr, of the Fyrdûr of Seerhold."

"Come, come!" Ama continued happily, leading her inside. "We have quarters for all, though not all have arrived."

Iltshyr spent another cycle waiting; they expected more than came, but had to start sometime. She reached the Hall of Council, but didn't enter; instead, she hesitated – her ears picked up an argument, one she wasn't supposed to hear, behind one of the Athenaeum's marble support columns – thusly, she studied a nearby mural, and listented:

"—not feel obligated to attend?" the voice was hushed, but laced with fury. She'd met this man before, the Thrush-King of Nûmundor, but he wouldn't remember. In truth, he was no King by blood or marriage, just a boy who built a city the misfits of the realms found, flocked to, and flourished in. They called him King, followed his law, and even claimed he could see the future. It was an odd little story, but the Fyrzhor considered him little more than a false prophet, a man of luck, rather than vision, and were impressed only with his inane charismatic godliness. Iltshyr's husband had cautioned her against the mind behind the eyes, as the Thrush-King's eyes swam in maneuvering, his tongue a constant influence. The Fyrdûr's words were of warning, and puzzlement: *'All in all, he's a good man ... I think ... but, there is a darkness in his heart we should not test.'* Now, in the Shadows of the colonnade, his lordly temper rose against a man of much smaller stature, a noble from the north by the sound of his accent. "Pray tell," the King spat, "What's more important to your nameless hero than the fate of a world? Than Aegis Herself?"

The accused, whoever he was, wasn't a fool; he brushed off the passing insult, "Love. With all due respect, my lord, the Nameless King led us to victory against Chaos. It was the end of a war for us, but the end of a lifetime for him, one he'd spent searching for his love. He freed her from the depths of bedlam's prisons, and I think the two of them deserve to rest in whatever happiness they've found together."

"Then, he is no King, nameless or not. A King would—"

Iltshyr heard all she needed to, and moved into the rippling-walled Hall of Council, symmetrically circular. There was no table, but she found a place reserved for her in the ring of thirty-three throne-like seats, matching the original thirty-three Myrmen. Today, thirty-two were in attendance, standing in the Shadows behind their respective places to leave room for those gathered; only Ama, first of them all, sat in the accommodation hewn for it. Of the missing Myrman, only Iltshyr knew the fate of it, and it would be one of her obligations to convey at this assembly what happened when the time came.

There were only thirteen representatives of the realms in all, save for their contingents left in quarters not privy to the fine points of the summit. The Thrush-King was last to enter, two little birds of his own name perched on either shoulder, whilst another whistled from his helm – it was strange, but Iltshyr was not one to question the avian familiarity. *Nature chooses who it will to follow, I suppose. Aegis has a plan for this prophet.* The Fyrzhor simply didn't know what it was, as finding out never took precedence over other priorities.

As the old man moved, Iltshyr saw every inch, every step pained him, until he reached his seat. Instead of sitting, he looked at them all and spoke far gentler than his quarrel outside indicated he would; still, there was an articulation of command with each syllable, trained perfectly so every ear would listen. "We have gathered to decide what is to be done with our world growing dark. Not once in our lifetime, or any others, have our races and cultures appeared like this, with a common cause, but never have we seen such loss, either. I have spoken with some of the gods, who call this the end of an age, and foresee that all things will pass under Shadow." There was a heavy disheartenment that pervaded the ring of mortals. The King raised a finger, "But, right now, I see faces I do not recognize, names I do not know, so..." he smiled, and a calm beset the air between them – a serenity that somehow touched and soothed their souls, "...as friends, let us begin with that – our names. I am Thane, Thrush-King of Nûmundor; whatever you know of me is true. That is all. And this..." he presented the man next to him.

"Is Tristlen," the man finished, standing. Both looked older than time itself, graying beards in bushels down to their chest, and armor ornately befitting their station, but exhaustingly used. "You won't have heard of me, though. I'm just a soldier. General to the Thrushmen, Captain of the Boughs Band, and I am humbly relieved to be standing here today."

Both men sat, so the next could stand. He was the nobleman arguing with Thane earlier, chiseled features cut similarly to the square, wool doublet he bore, embroidered silver. His hair was golden blonde, and his eyes bright blue, "I am Eoras, son of Aesyö. Hierarch to the Anvil City,

Protector of the Freemares, Steward over the Scars of Eurymyr, and this is Tithmus of Berth," he motioned to a man next to him, of comparable appearance, but a bit leaner, and dressed in fisherman's attire, "We speak for what remains of the Eurymyric Cities, and the Elderlands. I say this, as I see no Nithûr here to represent Barren or Highland."

No one claimed the contrary, so the next three around the ring roused as one, looking like nothing more than savages, clothed in animal pelts, with a mess of physical deformities brought on by deliberate scarring: "I am Ahtga, son of Ahtga, son of Ahtga, son of Ahtga, son of Ahtga, Chief of Lynxblood," the first said. Iltshyr blinked, and glared at Tithmus, who was finding it very difficult to keep his laughter behind closed lips. She recognized the Clansman's name; it was a line of some strange connection with Myrhaven itself, but she'd read it in some passing paragraph while waiting for the call to the chamber. She hadn't a mind to remember the details, now. He spoke with a much higher quality of learning than his kin.

As it was, the next mountain man growled quietly, "Öthel, son of Öther. Borrsblood." Iltshyr could tell this one had a hard opinion of things that would not be changed by outsiders.

The third was livelier, but rough around every edge, scarred in more places than not, "Goat, son of Ram, I dote, I am – heh! Master'a the Herdsblood, I be – see!" Iltshyr was lightly amused, but wondered if this was a conglomeration of kinships. *There has to be more clans than this down the Spine of the World...*

Next were two men of descent Iltshyr recognized, and loathed – Marchers, with their dark hair, sunbaked skin, and infamous hunting practices; they did it for pleasure, rather than purpose, and the Fyrzhor disapproved. They held ground far too close to the Cinderstride, and border skirmishes were numerous before the war began. Today, they were much worse for wear – dress tunics ripped, trousers stained, and boots bloody. "I'm Rakam," one said, "This is Lido." There was nothing but weariness in his voice, posture slunk, eyes hollow, "Titles're beyond us, now, but we volunteered to speak for what's left of the Marches in the south." He said no more, but eyed Iltshyr; she made them nervous, and it seemed they were truly broken of heart and soul.

Thus, it was to her. She stood as all others had, respectfully, "I am Iltvyrishyrdûr, of the Fyrzhor. I speak for the Cinderstride, and the Black-King Kirdûrikasdûmn." That was all she needed, so she sat back down. Saying less, always did more.

Next to her rose one familiar, and growing on her; he'd changed into fine linens with a wheat-stalk broach clasping a golden cloak, "I am Maleus, Croparch to Mistleton, Herald of the Wreatheland." Iltshyr couldn't help but notice the ire in Thane's eye; he wasn't happy to see this man alive at all. *He doesn't do well with cowards,* she thought.

A woman addressed them next, a gown of cerulean hues befitting her station reflecting her fair tone and fine stature, "I am Setya, daughter of Saryn the Fourth, Lady and Governess to the Coastal Cities in the west. I see no other Reignmen here, so I suppose I will speak for the Reignhearth as well. Sorrow fills me that Templeton has not seen fit to send an envoy."

"It's most likely gone to dust," this nihilism was from the last to speak, and one everyone had been eyeing warily since their arrival. It was hard to be still when a creature you could practically see through sat across from you. The Evendain, seen by fewer than even the Fyrzhor, were those who dwelt beneath the Stormstone Cascade, the depths of the Vein, and whose unbridled hatred for Seerhold would be tested today. It was a long, and bloody history, but one that went back nigh a thousand years to the Beginning. Iltshyr needed to be careful with this one. Setya sat, offering the floor, but the nearly translucent being, emblazoned with the silks and shimmers of his station, was the only one not to stand to address the council respectfully. However, he was abnormally cordial for one his kind, nonetheless, "I am Zain-evare Hyrök, one of six and six of one, Lord over and under the Evendûmn Hall." Iltshyr felt the shiver through the room. Before today, no one outside the Cascade may have ever seen an Evendain in person; it was a powerful tool, and he would surely use it to his advantage.

That was all of them, and Iltshyr noted as Setya did – there were no Reignmen; however, there were also no Elvar, no Eleaos'i, no Nithûr, no Baymen, and she wondered what was left of those parts of the world. *Can it truly be that bad? Could they all be dead?*

Ama presented its hand, palm up, "All of you were greeted by me, so to conclude this exordium I ask: Do we all heed to, and recognize, the voice of Thane, the Thrush-King of Nûmundor as moderator for this council at age's end?"

Ayes, nods, and grunts all around. It was he that brought them together, after all.

Thane nodded graciously, "Let us begin with the count. General?"

Tristlen straightened, but didn't stand – it would be a long day. "The count," he explained, "Is a good way to get our bearings. However, I see little point in starting with what we've lost, there is far too much of that. I will ask, instead, what have we left?"

One of the Myrmen stepped into the circle on cue, and rolled out the most beautifully intricate map of Aegis Iltshyr had ever seen, woven in a rug of greens, golds, reds, and blues. There were places on it that even the Fyrzhor knew not the names of.

"Nûmundor," Tristlen continued, "Stands, proud as ever. We erected Stonehall during the war, and plan on keeping it well provisioned, and well-lit through the night. You can see the Myrmen have already weaved its place into the threads of this tapestry."

"Mistleton," Maleus added, "Also survives. One bridge has been repaired, and we've sent our croppers out to begin sowing what they can. Unfortunately, there is nothing but ill tidings coming from the field. This Shadow may be poisoning the land."

Setya chimed in, "We've had the same problems across the 'Hearth. We don't think it's poison, but it's keeping us from planting. For the count, Reignberg endures, and we've begun to settle refugees on a few islands off the coast, there," she pointed. "It's doing very well."

"Isa," Ama motioned to one of its kin, "Please record the marks."

Another of the Myrmen, Isa, moved just inside the circle with needle and thread. Its fingers were the size of Iltshyr's thigh, and she found it a miracle the thing could hold the tools at all, let alone use them.

"Please, continue," Ama said.

"Well, Myrhaven survived," Eoras said in jest. "And a handful of Eurymyric cities were retaken by the Oisin after the Battle of the Divide. Orphaeon is among them, but ... things have changed within the very stone of it. A Shadow lingers there, so we have moved our capital to Berth."

Rakam sighed and shook his head, "How d'ya wish us to measure this, Nûmunyr? One could say Westmarch is still there, but only if ya count its rubble, or were a vulture. So's this really the best way of it? 'Cause in my eyes, the Marches are gone; let's start with that. All the forestry ya see there," he motioned to the map, "Along the Courseway – barren. It's all ash. All of it. A few hundred of us Marchers remain breathin' across where the water still runs clean, but there's a poison running through most of it turning our hopes worse 'an sour.

And I don't mean this confounded Shadow, I mean poison. From the blood and bile and bodies taintin' the banks at every turn. Most of us," his eyes shifted to the Clansmen, "Will be fleein' to the mountains, just hopin' to breathe air less putrid."

Everyone caught on, except for the Clansmen. Lido decided to help his fellow Marcher; he tried a more direct approach, "Will we be confronted by the Clans? Öthel? Ahtga? Goat? Can we sue for peace? We have nothing to barter, in trade or tribute."

Ahtga was the first to understand, "That's our mountain."

"We are only seeking a refuge."

Öthel spat, "Clans got no desire to harbor the weak."

"They'll not be weak," Rakam said warily, "But, they'll be unassumin', I assure you."

"I ain't promisin' nothing', Marchboy—"

Ahtga harrumphed, silencing him, and narrowed his eyes, "The Clans of the Spine will not," he looked from Öthel to Goat, "I repeat not, harm a peoples taking 'refuge' in our heights. But, yer peoples be warned this once, anyone seen as threat will be considered trespasser. If Blood-Chief claims this, they kill you on sight."

"And take your seed, yes indeed!" Goat added.

Lido saw the problem immediately, "Is there any way to know the Blood-Chiefs current territorial borders, so we may avoid any ... incidents?"

Öthel clenched his teeth, "Come too close—"

"We'll ask ya leave, ya? Ha!" Goat interrupted.

Ahtga nodded.

"And we'll do so, peacefully," Rakam said quickly; it was all they were going to get.

Tithmus piqued at this, "I think we can agree that any refugees, survivors, what have you, should all be welcomed by those here. To wherever their feet may find safety, I say. My little village of Berth will stand by this. No questions asked. Why not the same for those with larger quarter?"

"And if a Bayman appears at your gate?" this came from the Evendain, ominous and cold. Iltshyr heard something very wrong in the vibrations of Hyrök's voice, but she couldn't place it. Sure, they all knew the Baymen were allied with Chaos in the war, but what did that mean now?

Setya, as the Reignmen's loss was the greatest regarding the alliance between the Embers and the Twelfth, answered for him. "The servants of Syrsevar are all but eradicated; there will be no Bayman knocking on anyone's door. Ildûron was razed to the ground. Fyrzain is empty, but for the charred remains of traitors. Even Folly's Cove has been flushed out. I can tell you now, entire companies from the Divide have made sure of it, and any who survive are being hunted down as we speak."

"As it should be," Thane agreed. "All men reap what they sow."

Hyrök nodded.

Everyone knew it was extreme, but no one argued it. Therefore, Setya continued, "Adding to the count, there have been a dozen villages or so north and south of the Reignway that have sent jacks our way, but they exist only in fear." She chuckled awkwardly, "Some even ask if the Barony is still collecting taxes."

"Are they?" Maleus asked. There it was, Iltshyr saw it in his eyes, heard it in his voice – he used to be one of them, some sort of collector from across the Spine before finding his heart in the Wreatheland. Her fondness for him grew to genuine respect.

"No, Croparch," Setya snorted out his made-up title, "We aren't."

"Back to the point at hand," Eoras agreed with his northern friend, "The Eurymyric Cities will not just disappear into the night. The Elderlands is where what's left of the creatures of

Chaos still roam free. They no longer have direction, but they continue to kill anything that gets in their way of running. We will do now what we couldn't do then, and keep our people safe, no matter the cost. All survivors are welcome in Orphaeon as well."

Iltshyr caught the surge of blood pumping through the iridescent Evendain's veins, but again wasn't sure why. However, she was curious at the northerner's implicit vow, "I hear guilt in your voice, Hierarch."

Eoras looked down at his feet for just a moment, before swallowing, "I was searching for the Nameless King when Oisin fell to the fires of Chaos, and when my subordinates were forced to make a choice – kneel, or die. I do not blame them, for I was not there to guide their hand, but I will not fail them again."

"Where were you, Cinder Daughter?" this was Tristlen, Thane's General, who jumped at the follow-up. "We heard Seerhold had fallen."

There it was, finally. She took her time to answer, leaned back in the stone chair, "We lied." She admitted it freely, catching all the room off-guard. Now was the time to show her hand – a part of it, "We lied to you, because the Black-King knew exactly what you would do with it, and you did exactly that." She would not say the words, but the

Fyrdûr knew Thane hid a Heartstone in the vaults of Nûmundor to accompany, if not fuel, his visions.

The Thrush-King caught on quickly, and understood. He smiled warmly, "I'm glad you did, milady. Your little gambit worked. We turned the tide, you know."

Iltshyr returned the smile, fake as it was, "We heard." She frowned, leaning forward and gazing down at the map, "Ironically, Seerhold did fall, and only shortly after our lie. The abominations struck the tower, and flooded the Bellows. Then, at Fyrnûr Bay, we turned our tide as well." She paused to address Ama; they needed to know, "One of the *Myrain* was present," she reported. "It participated in the battle of Seerhold."

"Pa!" one of the stone-men exclaimed from Shadow.

Ama lifted its massive hand, "Settle, Kyra." They were shifting, murmuring all; whatever nerves they had running through their stone form were afire in the indifferent dark. "Yes. It was Pa."

"Its name?" Iltshyr asked, knowing the word in the ancient El'arria.

Ama nodded, "Reflected in the *myror*. Tell us what happened to it, Shyrdûr."

"Corruption. The Twelfth had ... done something to its mind, twisted it, defiled it, warped its purpose to a new one. One of destruction."

"And in the end?"

"The Ninth destroyed your kin. Stone to sand. I am sorry."

Ama stared at the floor; Iltshyr read the sadness furrowing its shingled brow, the grief ground between the aging cracks in its marble temple; she wondered if it could cry. Another of its kind appeared behind it, and gripped Ama's shoulder, "As only the Wrathlord could. We are glad. Nothing should live a slave to another, especially us, Ama."

Ama looked back up, "You are right, of course, Zhor. Many have fallen in this War of Shattering."

"But, many still live," Eoras added.

"And we should light the roads for them, yes?" this came surprising from Hyrök, and for a moment, no one knew how to respond.

Eventually, a few nods and murmurs of agreeance followed, even from the Clansmen, but it was Ama who spoke first, "After this, the Athenaeum will close. The gates of Myrhaven will shut forever. This is the last time any of you, or your scions, will see this place as it is, and us as we are."

There was a percolating rise of tension palpitating the hearts of all gathered. "What?" Eoras finally asked over his dumbfounded state, as the Oisin sent dozens of pilgrimages a year to the library.

"He means," Rakam answered for them, "That they're bowin' out. The Myrmen 'ave already come to their own conclusion, and it don't include any of us."

"You're giving up?" Setya asked.

"Yer practically gods," even Öthel argued it.

"Sods!" Goat was angry.

"Speaking of such, where are they?" Iltshyr caught Eoras say it under his breath. However, her eyes were trained on the Thrush-King – somehow, he was behind the Myrmen's decision, she knew it.

"Would it not be a sign of unity?" Hyrök pressed lightly.

The Thrush-King entered, now, "Yes, we should all know each other exists, come the day when it is needed we know, but I agree with the Myrmen. We should close our borders, strengthen our walls, and wait."

"Wait for what?" Setya asked.

"You're said to see the future, King of visions," Eoras' tone was built on frustration, rather than insolence, as the heat of their blood rose, "Do you see past the little sights of your Nûmundor?"

"I do," Thane said at length, patient as ever.

"What have you seen?" Setya wasn't sure what to make of the old man, but he intrigued them all.

Are we the only ones who know he has one of the raeordûmn? Iltshyr pondered.

Thane took his time, studying the individuals in the circle. The future was a slippery slope at best, and an *ogri's* avalanche at worst, when it came to revelation; there were so many possible interpretations, understandings, and erroneous assumptions. In the end, he sighed, "While I see beyond Nûmundor, I cannot see beyond this Shadow; I believe what futuresight I have is either diminishing with Aegis, or withdrawing," he admitted. "I cannot tell you which."

So many things were racing through their minds. "How convenient," Eoras broke the spell, "I say we can still band together to bring a light to this darkness."

"Agreed," Tirhmus added.

The Evendain nodded.

"No," Thane objected again.

"I don't believe this," Eoras was grasping at strands in the fatestreams, but Iltshyr knew there was no holding onto them.

"At least the lines of communication," Setya pressed.

"Right now," Thane stood, every muscle tense, every joint popping, "Right at this moment, whatever is happening out there is a mystery, one it is not the time to uncover. All we can hope to do is survive it. You've all said it – we're refugees, nothing more." Thane moved to the center of the circle, standing over the middle of the rug, where Templeton was threaded. He drove his finger down through the air as if to strike the tapestry, "We did not save a world, we have survived the death of one. Aegis has fallen. That is what I've called this council to say."

"You called us here to command us?" Hyrök's voice deepened, and there was venom there.

"You are the King of your Realm, not mine," Setya added.

"Clans rule mountain," Ahtga grunted.

"The Myrmen—" one of the Myrmen started from Shadow, but Ama rose its hand to stop its kin.

"I command no one, not even my own men," Thane rescinded. "I advise you, as I advise them. Years from now, maybe we'll see this Shadow lessened, even lifted on its own. But for now, it will remain what it is – a mystery."

"Have you seen this?" Lido asked.

"I have," he said this without hesitation, because he knew it was coming, and he couldn't have them question it.

"Then, who survives, survives," Hyrök changed direction, agreeing wholly, now. There was something in his opalescent skin, a flash in his corneas, an offbeat of his heart, Iltshyr did not trust.

Over the next hour, they finished the count – every known city and town across Aegis was checked off, either living, dead, or eviscerated. After sewing, ripping away, or modifying all as such on the map before them, it was recorded in ink, and the tome called *The War of Shattering and Origin's End*, was placed on the shelf of the Athenaeum's library.

However, Iltshyr knew what was wrong, and she was determined to see it through.

"You lied," everyone had gone to collect those they came with, except for the Thrushmen and Iltshyr. The self-proclaimed King stood in front of a wall, starring at the El'arria etched beautifully into the rock. Iltshyr had followed him in. She noticed some of the language had been rewritten, letters forged anew as all language changes in time. When Thane didn't respond, she repeated, not used to being ignored, "You lied."

"Apparently, we both do that, yes," he said gruffly.

"Why?"

"If I didn't say what I said, I feared much worse may've transpired here, and something more terrible than Chaos itself let loose."

Iltshyr thought about it. There was only one in that room who'd made her feel the same way, "The Evendain."

"The Evendain," he confirmed.

"In his heart."

"And eye. And soul. You could see it there, yes? Hidden. Zain-evare Hyrök did not come to see us, he came to study us."

"You think they would take advantage of this?"

"He wants the roads open; when have the people under the Cascade ever cared for open roads? Roads at all? They live under the bloody mountain!" Thane was letting the unknown get to him, "Better yet, ask yourself this – where were they?"

"What?"

"Everyone on the face of Aegis was fighting. The Elvar fought a few bouts in Chaos' fall; they harbored the Seventh. The Nithûr are still fighting in the Highlands, an unfortunate end to fire's retreat. The *Lûle'vitûm* itself was a front for the enemy; its people must have fought and died. Everyone has been in this war, but I didn't see a single one of those daemons on the battlefield, not in the west. I've spoken to Setya; there wasn't a single one on the Isdûn or in the Battle for the Divide. And I talked to the Eighth myself, who said they never broke the font into the Cascade. The Evendain did nothing. How do you miss a war of this magnitude? Naturally, I searched. I stared into the Heartstone of Nûmundor," the glint in his eye showed he knew the Fyrzhor were aware of not just the stones' presence, but that he admitted to having one in his possession. It was a risky confession, but he must've thought it imperative Iltshyr believed him, "And gave myself unto it to find them. Weeks, I was lost, but they were still hidden from me."

"How is that possible?"

"Your Fyrdûr and I both know, there's much of the *raeordûmn's* power we don't understand, but we know they have intent. They have conscious thought. Which means they have a plan, Cinder Daughter, as all things do. I'm afraid this plan does not align with Aegis', and I'm afraid they're using those closest to Her womb to see their will done."

"So, waiting is your way of watching, truly."

Thane nodded. "I will watch for as long as my eyes will open. Something festers in the Shadowgourge. One of my men – a knight,

Galaermus Galaborne – will use his dying breath to discover it."

"You claim to speak with the gods. What do they say about all this? Where are they? This is Mimyr's Athenaeum; where's Mimyr?"

"I speak with only those who wish to speak with me." He paused for a moment, and stared at her, "It's your god that did this, Fyrzhor." Thane went cold; he'd finally come around to the truth of his anger, "And you give him sanctuary. Stop asking me for my reasons and give me yours. He knew what would happen, we could have acted before Oisin fell, but he said nothing."

"Upon his sanctuary, he imposed self-exile, and knew not what was born of his mistake."

"He's a god. They may look like us, but their visage is where our similarities end. And yet, you harbor the father of Chaos himself, thinking you can save him?"

That was when she realized why she was here. Thane was plotting something. "No one can force the hand of gods, Thrush-King."

"I wouldn't dare." Thane was smart, and would not let her play with him, "Guilt is too powerful an ally. Go back with this, tell your Fyrdûr and warn your Wrathlord: Strengthen your borders, man your walls, and watch, because when the new age dawns, your gods will be gone from it, forsaken and forgotten." With that, he walked away, leaving Iltshyr alone in the inner sanctum.

The Thrush-King mounted his stallion, a gray and white speckled beauty. It nickered lovingly as he patted its muscled gullet, and ran his hands through its mane. It whinnied, and Thane responded, "Not yet, m'boy, we have another roundup before we're allowed to rest."

Eoras trotted up on one of the Freemares of the old Oisin Horselords. "Tell me something Thrush-King. If it weren't for this, all of this, what would you do with your life right now?"

Thane chuckled; he knew the Orphaeon noble meant well in the end, "Pass it to Aegis, I suppose. If I didn't have such a pressing desire to protect Her."

"And your visions – they're always right?"

"They always come to pass."

Eoras heeled his horse to come around Thane's other side. He stared the King in the eyes, this time with genuine respect. "I don't agree with you. I never will. But, if you hold any amount of respect for me at all, for my people, please, tell me, will the Eurymyr survive this?"

Thane reared his stallion, forcing Eoras' to hop back. "Eoras, son of Aesyö, named for the Eorlin of yore, I know this for certain: You are a good man. You did a good thing. You are truer than your Nameless King, and while I would never follow him into battle, I would follow you. To my knowledge, the Scars of the Eurymyr will never heal, but ... scars are there to help us remember. And you will be there to protect your people. Both of these things, in the end, will do the Anvil City proud, in whatever state it may find itself in. Keep an eye on that man of Berth, though, he may be greater than you."

"I seek not greatness or glory, only to be a good leader of my men."

"Then do as you did here. Never back down. Never surrender. And if you're the only one left, if you're the last chance, you win. You win, because there is no other way for Aegis to know you are Hers." With that, the Thrush-King galloped off, a contingent of Thrushmen following behind.

Anthology II

The Nameless

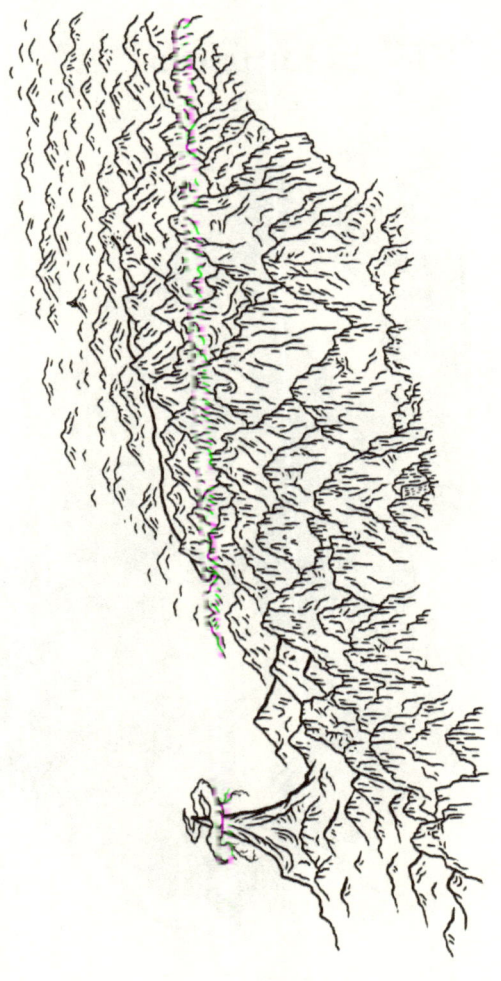

*...being a short story during the Age of Origin,
approximately in the year 972...*

Wizardry. Is that what it was? *No*, she thought. *She let me in, let me touch Her, let me use Her. But, why?* She'd reached the rise in the foothills, where boulders to bluffs were scattered in a rocky warren that led to the Stormstone Cascade – the mountains that stretched from the Spine east to continent's end. The heat was unbearable this afternoon, but a Nithûr's cloak breathed well, so she lowered its cowl against the blinding sun, welcoming what little shade it provided.

She ran her hand across the nearest boulder: *It was real, wasn't it? His blood was real. His death ... was real.* Her fingers found a shelf of moss hidden under a cleft in the rock, and, frustrated, pressed into the spores. Its nutrients exploded over her joints. *Was I Her soldier?* She ripped the migrant little clump from its refuge. *Was it some altruistic fight between good and evil? Right and wrong? Did She do it on purpose? Was it a mistake? I need to know!*

She wiped her hand on her robes, fingers stained with the death of life, and stared at it – like any other Nithûr's hand. She looked back the way she'd come from battle; she'd walked for miles across the Highlands' hills for days – feet like any other nomad's. And when she reached a shallow pool, maintained in a bowl of sediment dug between two rocks shaded from evaporation, she stared down at herself, trying to find some difference between the face in the reflection, and others who never had a chance in that useless war – her eyes were like any other woman's.

> She was not extraordinary.
> She was not special.
> She didn't know what to do.
> So, she wandered.

Eight days later, through the maze of stone populating the Cascade's crags, she saw the shepherd. He sat on a boulder sheered in half by some catastrophe centuries before. His tattered wools reached the ground, where his flock were scattered in a wide berth's radius around the knolls. His yellowed hair was thick, straight, but with a bushel of a beard; he was not haggard, but she felt he was older than he appeared. He was hunched over in thought or despair, she couldn't say which. When she closed in on him, she saw his crook at his feet, broken, split in two. *Despair, then, must be.* It was the simplest of shepherd's tools, but the most critical; without it, herding flocks and crossing long distances would be strenuous for any man half his age.

She knew how silently she carried herself, so she called forth her approach not to startle him, "Greetings, shepherd."

He raised his head, squinting against the sun, and waved, "Well met, traveler. Well met."

"This is not usually a place for sheep or their shepherds; may I ask?" She reached him, and stood between him and the sun.

He nodded, "Thank you, miss. And, how do I find myself here? Well, that Shadow and all, I feared it. So did my flock. Thus," he drummed on his legs – in which she heard an odd clanking sound – and looked about him, "We all tried a bit of moving. Now, I am afraid we are quite stuck, and the herd has grown a mind of their own. A salty, stubborn, reproachable one at that." There was a tempered bleating from behind a nearby slab. "Well, bring 'em back then!" he answered angrily.

The Nithûr woman held back a snort, "Is there anything I can do? I'm no good with sheep, I'm afraid."

There was an odd gleam in his eye when he caught hers again, "Not unless you can fix my crook," he said with a smile. "I haven't seen a good stick, or tree, for leagues to replace it or fashion a new one."

The Nithûr woman moved, leaned against a tall boulder next to his, and sighed, "I can't help you there."

"Ah, well," he shifted, and his robes fell open.

Beneath his tatters, she saw the most peculiar thing: *Armor?* *Cracked, old, rusting, but there... He can't be one of us.* "Are you one of us, shepherd? Of the Highlands? You look far too fair in eyes and hair."

The shepherd chuckled. "You caught me, miss. I don't roam east to west, no, but south to north."

"Across the Cascade?!" she was genuinely surprised. It was a long way, even without a herd of problem sheep.

"We thought these hills would lead our feet away from the layers of ash across the Wreatheland. But, alas..." he trailed off, needing to say no more.

It saddened her that this old man never found what he sought. "It seems the whole world's come to an end. I'm sorry." She looked down at his crook. "Such a simple thing, too." *Maybe I could... No. That was life and death. This is just a stick. I can't use Her for this.*

"Sometimes, I wonder," he said, scratching and stretching his jawline, "If we get lost, thinking that one place must be better than where we are, just because we have not seen it, and we take for granted just how important the little things are in the world. Gods know, I did. Life. Death. The big ones, you know. They make us fret and forget about what is in between." He laughed, softly, laced with a father's affection, "But, that's just an old man's opinion. Wishing he had done a little more smelling, and a lot less searching, if you know what I mean?"

The Nithûr chuckled, "Yeah, maybe." She knelt at the broken crook, paused, and thought about it: *If She doesn't want me to, She'll give me a sign, right?*

She removed her hood to bask in the heat. It warmed her, and she let that warmth strike a flint to spark a fire through her pores. She caressed the crook, feeling every twist of the wood, listening. She focused on where it felt raw, before it was whittled to perfection. *The age!* That knowledge arrived first in her mind. *So old...* The crook was ancient, hewn from a tree far from the land she knew, where a forest was no more than a sparse glade in her eyes' mind; this wood grew naturally smooth, no need for the tools of man. She moved her hand from knot to little knot, each tiny twist had a purpose, a direction it desired to grow—

Fire!

Lightning!

Crack!

It had split from battle, but an unnatural one, and recently. She focused, focused on the nature of it. The machination of fire and forge would not do here. That was life, and that was death. But this, she harnessed it – *It's growth!* she realized. Growth was what she needed here. She recalled her childhood, when she ran barefoot across the hills, felt the grass between her toes, and she allowed that soft embrace to carry her to a bed of fanciful fruition on a cloudy Rhiltyr day. She thought back on cliffs, cliffs she couldn't scale, inches away, until years passed, and she was up the mountain. She thought of young infatuations, obsessions over a face, a lock of hair, an arm of strength, all fading away to affection based on understanding, connection, true love. Her hands moved the halves of the crook together, and she clutched them tight with one. *Root,* she thought, *I need to find the root.*

Her free hand went down to the flesh of Aegis. *Please...* She found the soil soft, welcoming. She sank her fingers into the earth, and let her mind slip away, through her body, and into the world.

Roots. She found them by the thousand, the million. Acres of underground where one appeared no different than the other – *Idiot!* she reprimanded herself. *They are different. Of course, they're different. Like the peoples above, they are the civilization below.* She caught the hint of a voice, and followed it. *A willow!* Amidst a forest untouched by the fires of Chaos, it was a willow that cared for others, a mother in an estuary, a sanctuary, whose roots grew long and wild to support her sons and daughters down a dozen banks; she was singing to her children against the Shadow looming over them all.

> *Ah-ah-ah-oh, Ah-oh-ah,*
> *Ama nir dûm ûmn-i*
> *Rör iö-i ihn söm*
> *Ama nir dûm umn-i*
> *Ah-ah-ah-oh, Ah-oh ah,*
> *Mmh, mmh, mmhmm...*

The Nithûr moved on, the willow wasn't old enough. She passed roots burnt, decaying, and dead, roots reaching in vain for a vein of water, fighting hair and tissue to survive the same war that rent across the face of Aegis without mercy for nigh on forty years. The suffering above was not enough it seemed, as so much below was still travailing just for a taste of basic nutrients. She spat the taste of death from her mouth and mind: *I have to focus!* And she did – on the living, the flourishing, the first – and found it!

Under a wide river, then up to a small island set at its center, there was a root that led not just to one tree, but the eldest family of flora in existence. Brothers and sisters in arms sprouted from the same seed, connected through miles of womb, and its bast held the fibrous design of the shepherd's crook. She felt the bond flow through her, grab hold of her, then kick back – her command over the pieces of staff intensified. She felt water pour from her palms, seeds pop from her pores, and spores feather out amidst slivers of bark from the heartwood of this ancient isle.

Her eyes snapped open, and soil fell like rain as nature's tears from her ducts. She watched her hand; it blossomed with petals between her fingers at first – they wrapped around the crook's shaft like swaddling clothes. Next came the vines, vines that eagerly enveloped the crack, tightening its halves together, until:

    Shower!

                    Seed!

        Flower!

                        Seal!

The shepherd's crook was whole again.

The Nithûr woman and the shepherd sat there in silence, until her curiosity got the best of her, "Your walking stick is ... unique?"

He smiled, "It was a gift. As everything else Aegis gives us." He stood with the help of the crook, and whistled. A few of his closest flock trotted up.

"Where are you going, now?"

"Here. There."

"And in between?" she thought back to what he'd said before.

"Yes. The in between will be nice, I think. What matters is how we go, do you agree? Not where we go."

She cocked a wry grin of insight, "How we grow, you mean."

He raised a finger, "Now you are starting to understand." He began walking away, his bleating troublemakers following behind. Before the shepherd-soldier disappeared over the hill, he called back, "And all will grow around you, my dear, I believe. That is, if you believe. All will grow around you."

Anthology II

Other works released under Canticles Productions

Canticles Mythos Series
Volume I: The Age of Origin
Anthology I: The First Sires
Anthology II: The First Fallen
Anthology III: The First Fires (forthcoming)

Canticles Children Series
Sybil and the Floot-Snoot (July, 2020)

Canticles Literature Series
Poet's Compendium I: Hand in Hand (forthcoming)
The Return of the Wren (forthcoming)

Canticles Albums
Aria I: The Heroes of Our Days
Aria II: The Shadows of Our Past
Aria III: The Nature of Our Love (forthcoming)
The Life and Lore of Winterstide (forthcoming)
Faerû's Lullaby [Single]
The Öleander's Kiss [Single]
The Pursuit of Stars [Single]
To Follow a Broken Heart's Beat [Single]

on PATREON

Canticles' vision took flight in the Summer of 2016,
and is now a Patreon-Based, independent Production
Company.

A little about us:
We're based in the Midwest, not Hollywood.
We offer originality, not rehash and remakes.
We are family-friendly, and have something for everyone!

Join the adventure today!
Be a part of the Canticles Family!
Become a Patron at:
www.patreon.com/canticlesproductions

ISBN 978-0-692-16868-4

9 780692 168684